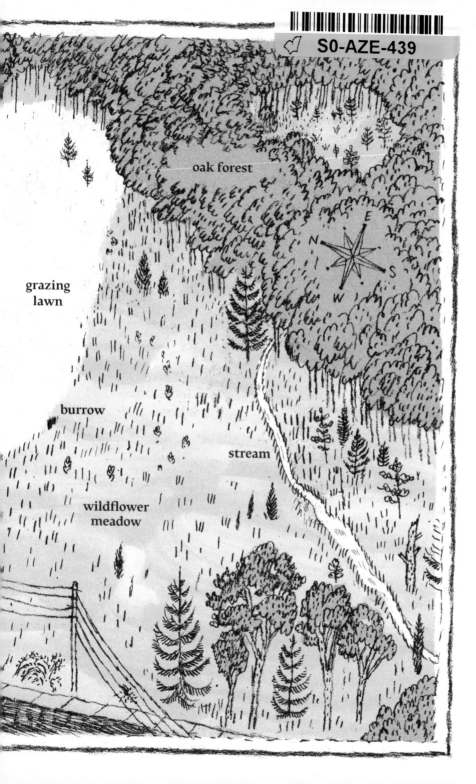

oak forest

grazing
lawn

burrow

stream

wildflower
meadow

The
Remarkable Rescue
at Milkweed Meadow

The Remarkable Rescue *at* Milkweed Meadow

Elaine Dimopoulos

Illustrated by
Doug Salati

🏠 Charlesbridge

Published by Charlesbridge
9 Galen Street, Watertown, MA 02472
(617) 926-0329 • www.charlesbridge.com

Library of Congress Cataloging-in-Publication Data
Names: Dimopoulos, Elaine, author. | Salati, Doug, illustrator.
Title: The remarkable rescue at Milkweed Meadow / Elaine
    Dimopoulos; illustrated by Doug Salati.
Description: Watertown, MA: Charlesbridge, 2023. | Audience: Ages 8
    and up. | Audience: Grades 4–6. | Summary: "Butternut is a young,
    anxious rabbit and master storyteller who makes friends outside
    her burrow—even though she was cautioned not to—and now must
    decide whether she will remain loyal to her family or help other
    animals in need."—Provided by publisher.
Identifiers: LCCN 2022012789 (print) | LCCN 2022012790 (ebook)
    | ISBN 9781623543334 (hardcover) | ISBN 9781632893062 (ebook)
Subjects: LCSH: Rabbits—Juvenile fiction. | Meadow animals—
    Juvenile fiction. | Animal rescue—Juvenile fiction. | Storytelling—
    Juvenile fiction. | Friendship—Juvenile fiction. | CYAC: Rabbits—
    Fiction. | Meadow animals—Fiction. | Animal rescue—Fiction.
    | Storytelling—Fiction. | Friendship—Fiction. | LCGFT: Animal
    fiction. | Novels.
Classification: LCC PZ7.1.D566 Re 2023 (print) | LCC PZ7.1.D566
    (ebook) | DDC 813.6 [Fic]—dc23/eng/20220425
LC record available at https://lccn.loc.gov/2022012789
LC ebook record available at https://lccn.loc.gov/2022012790

Printed in the United States of America
(hc) 10 9 8 7 6 5 4 3 2 1

Illustrations created in graphite and gouache and completed digitally
Display type set in Desire by Charles Borges de Oliveira
Text type set in Elmhurst by Christopher Slye
Printed by Maple Press in York, Pennsylvania, USA
Production supervision by Nicole Turner
Designed by Diane M. Earley

For Athena, my little female human

I.

Everyone in Milkweed Meadow still talks about the rescue, and if you stop hopping around like a kit that's found a banana slice, I'll tell you the story. Mother encourages strong beginnings. "Snare them!" she says. It's a joke—we rabbits are terrified of snares, me more than most. But I suppose that's what a good story does. It digs into your skin like a silver wire and holds you in its grasp.

I could begin the day Winsome crashed into our home and broke her leg, or the day I met Piper and nearly toppled off the trellis. But I'll go back further, to Blue—at his most despicable. I'm glad I was busy in the burrow at the time. Even so, I can imagine exactly how he and his dark heart carried out the misdeed.

The first thing you need to know is that Blue ruled the feeder at the neatly mowed grazing lawn next to the meadow. He'd always ruled it. He flapped like a storm at the chickadee brothers if they approached while he was eating. "Stay away, or I pluck you clean!" he'd shout at the house sparrows and the other small birds, seed crumbs exploding from his beak. The woodpeckers were the only ones that sometimes squawked back, but that big bully always held his ground. Even the squirrels shot away to the oak trees when he dove at them.

Blue's something to look at, all right. My fur is the color of wet wheat. Mother wouldn't like that I don't express pride in my appearance, but I've always envied the piercing blue feathers of jays, with their black-and-white dappling. I'm not the only one, either, because when he feeds, two faces often appear at the window of the house next to the lawn. The little humans who live there, the ones who fill the feeder with seed whenever it runs low, love to watch him, I've noticed.

It seems wrong that a creature so beautiful could be so vile.

The cruelest thing that day was that Blue must have been full already after a morning of eating. He'd hopped off the feeder—but instead of performing his usual midday calisthenics in the trees, he decided to peck around on the ground near the mourning doves.

The poor doves. Mother says they aren't very smart. I don't know if I agree with her, but they have gentle natures. They eat fallen seed and stay out of everyone's way.

Blue fixed his black eye on one of the doves and hopped toward him. The dove hopped away obligingly. Again Blue advanced. The dove retreated. They continued this slow dance under the feeder, Blue never doing anything more than staring and hopping in pursuit.

Finally the dove couldn't take it. "What do you want?"

Blue tilted his head so his other eye beheld the dove. "Name?"

"Culver."

"Just looking at you, Culver. Getting to know you. We're not friendly enough in Milkweed Meadow, is my opinion."

Culver looked at the other doves for help, but they responded with nervous twitches. He shook his head and tried to continue eating under Blue's scrutiny. "Oh, hen's teeth," he muttered at last, and flew off like a gray stone flung into the sky.

"Leave them in peace, Blue." The voice came from above, high and crisp, and the birds and squirrels looked up to see a robin circling. It was Mother First-fledge.

"I do what I please," Blue called back.

"Yes, you do, and we all suffer. Why don't you migrate and find some other flocks to torment?" Preferring worms and bugs, the robins didn't have to put up with Blue's bullying at the feeder. Maybe that's what gave Mother Firstfledge courage.

"Watch your beak," said Blue, "or you'll be sorry, is my opinion."

"You don't scare me." She swerved and flew away over the top of the house.

Blue stood quietly for a moment. He must have been aware of the eyes on him, the others waiting to see his reaction. I don't know if he was driven by wickedness, or the need to back up his words, or some ugly mix of both.

The robins had built their nest near the house, on the crossbars atop the wooden trellis. It was nestled cozily under a gable. Blue flew to the top of the trellis and perched next to the nest.

We had all overheard the robins talking about how proud they were of their four eggs that spring.

Blue snatched one of the eggs in his mouth and flew to the ground. Beak slightly parted, he tapped at the shell until it cracked. I don't have the stomach to dwell on what came next, but there—right there on the lawn in the late morning sunshine—the feathered brute feasted.

II.

"Stop quivering. Bird affairs are *not* rabbit affairs!"
Mother had been lecturing in the root room when one of my aunts burst in and told us the gruesome news. It took a while for Mother to calm my brothers and sisters and me. I eventually stopped hopping up and down in anguish, but I couldn't quiet my mind. It grew brambles that kept scrabbling toward the prickliest possible outcomes, as it always did. *What if Blue eats the eggs of every bird in Milkweed Meadow? What if there are no more birds around to eat beetles and caterpillars? What if they multiply and eat the plants? What if the whole meadow is destroyed?*

I didn't like the empty feeling in my belly if I came late to dinner. What would I do if we starved?

5

The root room is a large gathering space in the burrow with a domed dirt ceiling woven with tree roots. From her lecture mound, Mother rose onto her hind legs. "Kits! Enough! Blue has no *dignity*," she declared. "What do you expect?" In a stern voice she reminded us that birds were a primitive class of animal. Egg-layers, after all. We were to keep our heads down during breakfast and dinner on the lawn and worry about the burrow-dwellers *only*.

I couldn't keep my fears to myself. "But what if Blue eats another egg?" I squeaked. "What if he keeps eating eggs? Do you think there would be a bird battle? Would we take sides? Would we have to shelter in the burrow? How would we get food? How—"

"No one's going to battle!" My brother Kale eyed me with that exasperated look I'd come to know well. "The robins still have three eggs left, after all. Let Mother finish her lecture." Kale was the eldest, the one who always succeeded at everything he tried, who always did everything first. He helped the rest of us . . . but sometimes I wondered if he could ever truly understand me.

My sister Goosegrass pressed her body lightly into my side. "The robins will be on the lookout for Blue now, at least," she murmured.

But they have to sleep sometime! I wanted to squeal. Instead, under Kale's admonishing gaze, I forced myself to nod.

I liked Goosegrass because she never laughed when I told her about my fears. Once, when the lawn sprinklers were left on overnight, I worried aloud that if the grazing lawn flooded, the water could seep into the meadow and drown us, since our burrow bordered the lawn. "That would be terrible," Goose-grass admitted, snuggling closer to me in the slumber nest. "Though if we're going to drown, I'd rather be asleep. G'night, Butternut."

As you know, the meadow didn't flood.

And why, yes, Butternut *is* my name!

I suppose it might be a male rabbit's name. I happen to be female. My grandmother Sage began the tradition of naming the members of our colony after plants rabbits like to eat. My mother is Nettle. My sisters are Lavender, Clover, Thistle, Goosegrass, and Baby Sweetcorn, and my brothers are Kale, Chicory, Watercress, and Mallow.

Your name sounds funny to my ears too, you know!

Back in the root room, Mother did eventually return to her lecture that day. I believe she was talking about how to keep the dialogue in our stories snappy, but my mind was so full of pictures of broken eggs that I can't be sure.

Blue's audacity kept me in a daze until we left the burrow for our colony's evening meal. I looked for him, despite Mother's warning to keep my head down. I couldn't help it. Even though he frightened me, I wanted to see what a criminal's face looked like. But Blue had made himself scarce.

I glanced up at the robins' nest. One of the robins was sitting on the remaining three eggs, facing away from the lawn. From its tail feathers, I couldn't tell if it was Mother or Father Firstfledge.

While we chewed grass on the lawn, a couple of house sparrows grazed quietly at the feeder. Squirrels sniffed for acorns around the lawn and meadow.

No one spoke to the robin.

At the end of the day, our slumber nest is usually a comforting place. Mother doesn't mind that it's coated with fur and that our hoarded playthings, sticks and pretty stones, are scattered everywhere. My siblings and I all pile together in a cozy heap. Some nights Baby Sweetcorn leads us in mischief-making until Mother appears in the entryway and scolds us. Other nights, sleep makes our heads stone heavy and we drift right off—but not before hearing a story. We go in order, one storyteller per night.

That night it was Mallow's turn. After the chaos of the day, I was looking forward to a distraction, but Mallow had Blue on his mind. Kale quieted us all and told him to begin.

"One day Blue decided he wanted to be an artist," Mallow said. "He began to sculpt a statue of himself out of twigs and string. In his small heart, he found unexpected joy in creating something where nothing before had been. He spent hours on his work. But the wind remembered Blue's crime. It blew ferociously, scattering raindrops, bending the brush, and swaying the trunks of trees. Blue was roosting when it hit. He flapped his wings, fighting the stormy gusts to get to his sculpture. He arrived in time to see the woven twigs burst apart and shower the meadow with a patter. He wailed in dismay and let the wind carry him away."

Mallow snickered once he'd finished.

"Points for drama," murmured Lavender. "But Mother would say you've cast Blue as the hero, not the villain. We feel sympathy for him, and the truth is, he deserves none. G'night."

Long after I heard deep breathing around me, I was still thinking about rogue winds cutting through the meadow and forest, ripping off branches and toppling trees so that their roots poked upward like gnarled parsnips. And we rabbits, huddling in the burrow, praying for the wrathful storm to end.

Funny. The rescue took place on a night a little like the one in Mallow's story. Our greatest fears can indeed come to life. And when we face them, they're scary—but sometimes in a completely different way than we expected.

III.

So now you know just how awful Blue was. Any questions?

What's that? Well, *you* sit in a classroom and have lessons, don't you? What's so odd about rabbits doing the same thing?

I'll explain. Each morning after breakfast, my brothers and sisters and I shuffle down to the root room. Three generations of rabbits have hopped across its dirt floor and packed it firmly. We arrange ourselves in staggered rows. Before our midday naps and dusk feedings, we receive education.

Receiving education is a tradition in my family. Teaching us is mainly Mother's job now, but Grandmother Sage started it all. She tells us her story whenever she's not feeling sleepy. Before we get to the rescue, you should hear it too. Don't worry—it has a happier ending than the robins' egg story.

There was once a pet rabbit named Bun Bun, who roamed inside a human house during the day and slept in a cage at night. Some humans had found Bun Bun as a baby Eastern cottontail. She remembers feeling cold and then waking up warm in a place with strange smells and eager faces peering at her. The humans gave her liquid from a dropper. They touched her sometimes, but when she trembled, they stopped.

She rode in a vehicle to visit another human called a wildlife rehabilitator. On the way, the smallest human held up her carrier, and she stared out the window at the houses and trees. The wildlife rehabilitator pricked her with a silver barb—then, surprisingly, talked to the humans about her health and healing. There were other injured animals in his dwelling; most smelled dangerous, and some made noises that frightened her. One, a bat, opened an eye and grinned at her before returning to sleep.

The rehabilitator said it was against human laws to keep her inside a house. He said it firmly. Smiling, the humans promised to release her into the woods. When they returned home, they put her in her cage to rest and shut the house doors, including the latch on the old dog door. Firmly. Then, they named her.

Bun Bun listened to the humans, who talked a lot. She perked up her sizeable ears when they brushed her and learned about harmful mites and ticks. She listened when they fed her and learned the names of plants rabbits can eat, like dandelion and parsley—and some, like rhubarb, that they can't.

Most of all, Bun Bun listened while the larger humans read stories to the smaller ones. Bun Bun heard one story about a rabbit escaping from a garden and leaving its blue jacket behind. Another about a rabbit that lives in a briar patch and outsmarts a fox. Yet another about a stuffed rabbit in a nursery that receives so much love it becomes real. So many rabbits, having so many adventures. She heard stories about other animals too—dogs, mice, bears, cats— and about humans. At night she would lie awake. In her mind the bars of her cage would melt, and her heroes and their worlds would take form around her.

One night, nervously, she tried her paw at telling a story. "Once upon a time there was a rabbit in a cage," she whispered into the empty room. She remembered that details make a story more specific. "Her name was Bun Bun. Her ears were long. Her white tail was spotlessly clean." What next? So many of the stories the humans read seemed to get at some sort of truth. "The humans in her house cared for her, but she wondered what it would be like to live near other rabbits. She was lonely." With this admission Bun Bun fell silent. She'd hit upon a truth, and it hurt.

It didn't take long for the attentive rabbit to observe exactly how the closure on her cage fastened and unfastened.

She tried it one night with her teeth, and it opened straightaway. Frightened, she closed it again and sat quietly, thinking. The next day she ate a double serving of lettuce, drank plenty of water, and napped.

That night she left. Down the stairs she crept, cautiously, and nudged open the latch on the flapping dog door. *Perhaps the humans will get a dog now,* Bun Bun thought. She emerged into the cold night. The moon shimmered like a lunaria blossom. As she hopped along the side of the road, she kept watch for the lurking predators from the stories. Owls, snakes, foxes, badgers. She focused on her destination: the house with the tasty-looking lawn a few miles away. She'd seen it from the vehicle window. It was near a wildflower meadow, beyond which a little stream ran. And beyond that, curling around the property like a hug, an oak forest.

She hopped all night, ignoring her body's sleep cravings. Despite her fortitude, she saw something unspeakable on her journey. It involved a pack of lean coyotes with high-pitched, piercing wails. The stories were true: villains existed. She was deathly afraid.

We kits had all been warned not to ask about the details of this part of the story because they were too frightening to share. Naturally my brambles made me brood on the darkest possibilities: *Did the coyotes lunge out of the brush? Did they chase a creature? Did they catch it?*

Whatever happened that night, Bun Bun survived. By dawn she'd reached the meadow. She ate a few mouthfuls of clover, dug a hollow with her remaining strength, and slept for hours.

When she awoke, she decided that she couldn't possibly begin her new life as Bun Bun, so she took the name Sage. She found an abandoned groundhog den where the meadow met the lawn. Though her species is usually territorial, Sage craved companionship—and saw other advantages to colony living. Her offspring helped her expand the den into a branching burrow. The females stayed to teach and lead. The adult males eventually left to roam over a larger range, but they never forgot what they learned there.

Grandmother taught her kits three things, which they now teach their kits.

1. Stories Matter

Interesting characters. A thorny conflict. A wood-gnawing climax. Details that let you smell and taste and touch. Grandmother Sage never forgot the stories she heard in the humans' house. She calls them her salvation. Every rabbit in Milkweed Meadow must learn the art of storytelling.

Not every story we tell has to be about rabbits, of course. Some can be factual, and some can be pulled from the colorful gardens of our imaginations. But all must have truth at their core.

For truth is what made Grandmother Sage know she needed to escape the human house. When we tell a story, we share something that feels like truth to us, and other rabbits get to consider it. Stories entertain, but they connect us too.

And when a story *doesn't* ring true, well, you know it's time to try it again.

We practice telling our stories in the root room, when we curl up in the slumber nest at night, when it rains, anytime we can.

I'm practicing on you right now.

2. Rabbits Have Dignity

Grandmother Sage's theory is that humans wouldn't have invented so many stories about rabbits unless they held a special place in the world. She taught us that we are attractive mammals with backbones and sharp senses—higher-order creatures. That we must respect ourselves and our colony.

Therefore grooming matters. Partly to show self-respect, but also to get rid of any mites or bugs that could make us sick. Grandmother Sage remembers how thorough her grooming in the house used to be. Her special tools are a secret of the colony. Over time she risked her life to steal a few old, broken comb and brush bits from the humans' garbage. Her most valued possession is a metal hair comb with a gold dragonfly above the teeth. She keeps it in the grooming room, but the rest of us know not to use it if anything else is available.

Once a day we each hold a comb in our teeth and give one of our sisters or brothers a thorough brush down, paying special attention to the hindquarters, as Mother instructs.

3. Stay Alive

We must also preserve ourselves and our colony.

Grandmother Sage named Milkweed Meadow. The milkweed plant, with its puffy blooms, is plentiful around our burrow. The name caught on among the other animals, even those that don't live in the meadow proper, as we do. But they don't know the full story.

Most animals can't eat milkweed, because its sap contains a poison—but monarch caterpillars can. When these caterpillars turn into butterflies, birds and other animals that would ordinarily love to chomp on insects avoid monarchs because the milkweed in their systems makes them toxic to eat.

Grandmother decided that since we rabbits didn't have a food to make us invincible, we needed to use our heads. *Our milkweed is our brainpower,* she was fond of saying in a solemn voice. I didn't know if rabbit brains worked differently from other creatures' brains, but with smart habits, she believed we could increase our survival odds.

Grandmother chose to live near the kind of humans who are happy that we nibble their plants, instead of the kind who set snares with silver wires.

She and Mother taught us to avoid risks. *Stick together. Don't go out after the sun sets. Don't journey too far into the forest. Don't drink from the part of the stream where the water rushes by quickly. Don't talk to other creatures unless you have to. Quiet your voices around humans—we understand them, but we don't want them getting curious about us. Never trust humans fully. They keep rabbits as pets, after all.*

Use your milkweed, Grandmother told us, *and you'll stay alive.*

Also, every rabbit in the colony must learn to cross the road in front of the house. Having ridden in a vehicle, Grandmother Sage knows how dangerous they are to rabbits. She feels confident we can use our excellent hearing to tell when a vehicle is coming and when it is safe to cross.

I have excellent hearing, and I was still terrified of crossing the road. I kept putting off my road test. My mind's brambles led to dreadful endings where I got crunched like a pine cone or splattered like a winterberry. As you can see, though, I'm still here.

I hope you can also see why the tale of Grandmother Sage escaping captivity is considered one of the burrow's most captivating stories. It used to be my absolute favorite—until Goosegrass and I turned an adventure involving Grandmother's gold dragonfly comb into a thrilling new story. One that I had to wait a long, long time to tell.

It was this comb—and Blue's nasty spitefulness—that transformed a quiet evening in Milkweed Meadow into a whole droppings pile of a mess.

IV.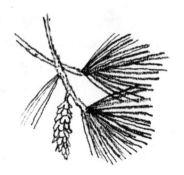

About a week after Blue ate the robin egg, my sister Goosegrass was in trouble. Why she was in trouble barely matters because she was always in trouble. Do you know humans like that?

Goosegrass was always oversleeping. Always losing track of time. Always late to the root room. Never prepared with her lessons. Her paws forever dusty or muddy.

The stories she told meandered and sometimes didn't make sense. Grandmother Sage came into the root room to hear our presentations that day. The air was still and warm; I suppose Mother liked it this way because there were no buzzes or chirps or sweet-smelling breezes to distract us.

As usual Mother put Goosegrass near the end of the order. I believe that was the morning my sister told us all a story about a stone that was magically turned into a rabbit but decided it preferred life as a stone. Mother couldn't hide her exasperation. "You are talking to an audience of *rabbits*," she declared. "What kind of connection are we supposed to make with your hero?"

"You have a unique voice, Goosegrass," said Grandmother Sage, a hint of a smile softening her face. "Your story seemed to miss its truth this time."

"Okay." Goosegrass shrugged. "Stones seem pretty happy as stones though."

Grandmother's smile turned into a chuckle. "Keep practicing."

Mother told Goosegrass she had to revise her story before she could go to dinner that night.

The extra work made her late to dinner. My brothers and sisters were heading in as she was coming out, but I stayed on the grazing lawn to keep her company. We had left behind spring's soggiest days, and delicious white clover was beginning to bloom everywhere as the temperatures rose. We appreciated that the humans in the house didn't behead this delicacy when they mowed.

As I pulled up an extra mouthful, I noticed a movement in the forest. Whatever it was herked and jerked, this way and that, unlike any creature I'd seen. There was something misshapen and unnatural about its body. I sat up, still as a lawn statue, and whistled to Goosegrass.

"Stay alive," I said. "Back to the burrow."

We heard an unmistakable call for help.

The voice sounded squirrelish. I hesitated, and suddenly the scampering oddity bolted across the meadow and popped into view on the lawn.

I recognized the two squirrel siblings, though I didn't know their names. A male and a female. Their tails were stuck together. When they both ran forward, they did all right, but when one tugged in a certain direction, the other would get knocked off its feet, scrabble to right itself, and tug in the opposite direction.

"Pine sap!" the female called out. "We'll be stuck like this forever! Please help us!"

"Does it hurt?" asked Goosegrass.

The female tried to shake her tail free, but the angry tangle just seemed to tighten. The male squirrel burst into fresh tears.

"Very, very much," said the female.

I felt bad, but squirrels weren't burrow-dwellers. We didn't owe them help. I was wondering how to express sympathy and retreat to the burrow before the miserable creatures attracted a hungry fox or owl. "Could your parents untangle you?" I asked politely. "Or one of your brothers or sisters, maybe?"

"They could use one of our combs!"

Goosegrass's lack of sense made me want to explode at her. I gritted my teeth. "I don't think—"

"What's a comb?" the female squirrel asked.

"I'll get one!" Goosegrass raced into the burrow.

The squirrels and I looked at each other. The male's cries diminished to whimpers. "I'm Inka," the female said after a pause. "This is Twain."

"Oh. I'm Butternut." I glanced skyward. "Perhaps we should hide?"

We ducked under a holly bush. The squirrels couldn't stop twitching and scratching at the ground. Mother had taught us the term *rodents*, but I tried not to think about the stories of plague and pestilence she'd shared. Finally Goosegrass sprinted out of the burrow with something in her teeth.

Wouldn't you know it? It was Grandmother Sage's dragonfly comb.

"Have you lost your senses?" I hissed as she joined us under the bush.

"Ips teef are feh sharpesht," Goosegrass replied, her mouth full and grinning.

"Fine. Let me." I snatched the comb from her. Goosegrass was about as good at grooming as she was at storytelling.

While the squirrels gasped in agony, I attacked the tangle with tiny tugging movements of the comb's teeth. The sap was sticky, and I ripped more than I untangled, but slowly, slowly, the two tails began to separate. The large sap ball at the tip looked like a pebble of honey, so I worked the teeth on either side of it. Gradually the hairs gave way, and the pebble detached. At first the squirrels couldn't move for the pain. Their faces were twisted and their eyes squeezed closed. Goosegrass hopped back and forth, gamely patting their paws.

But it did feel good when they eventually opened their eyes and shook their tails independently. Inka's face broke into a smile. "We're free, we're free, we're free!" she exclaimed. "You did it!"

When he discovered his own freedom, Twain began sprinting around the lawn, running up and down tree trunks, and shaking his patchy tail.

Breathing hard, he returned to the holly bush and surprised Goosegrass and me by kissing our cheeks. Being touched by a creature other than a rabbit felt mostly nice and only a tiny bit dangerous. He was a sweet thing.

"What a pretty trinket, is my opinion."

The voice was unmistakable. Goosegrass froze. The two squirrels dashed into the meadow as if wasps had stung their hindquarters.

Blue alighted on the ground next to the holly bush and tucked in his wings. "Two rabbits, two squirrels, and a dragonfly, all playing together. How come nobody invited me?"

I'd never stared Blue in the face before. From where we crouched, his eyes looked like nightshade berries. His beak like a thorn. His coloring was so rich, so unnatural that it made him seem like a creature of legend from one of Grandmother's stories.

He stood between us and the burrow entrance. I wasn't sure what he'd do if we made a dash for it. I'd never been pecked before. *This* was why Mother and Grandmother told us to use our milkweed, keep our heads down, and concern ourselves with rabbit affairs.

I tried to steady my voice. "We were just going home, Blue."

He ignored me. "So the rabbits have a secret treasure. Give it here."

Grandmother's comb lay on the grass near my paws. Goosegrass and I looked at each other. I wasn't sure what was worse, getting pecked or losing the comb to Blue. No matter how well I told the story, Mother was sure to punish me alongside my foolish sister.

"Sorry. It's Grandmother's," said Goosegrass courageously. "We're not allowed to share it."

"So you share it with the squirrels but not with me," Blue squawked. "Unfair, is my opinion." Quick as a snake, he snatched the comb in his beak, opened his wings, and flew to the top of the trellis. He was close to the robins' nest, and the prospect of broken eggs made me quiver from nose to tail.

Ignoring the nest, Blue dropped the comb onto one of the wooden crossbars. It wobbled and lay still, twinkling in the low evening sunlight. "Let's see your grandmother comb her pretty fur now." He threw his head back and cackled before flying off into the treetops.

V.

Now I'm going to try to keep the pride out of my voice when I tell this part of the story. You're probably thinking that the comb was lost to Goose-grass and me for good. Or that if we got it back, it was due to chance: a breeze blew it off the trellis, or Mother or Father Firstfledge knocked it down with their wings.

You'd never think that I, Butternut, performed a daring one-rabbit recovery mission!

I'll tell you where my courage came from. It came from righteous indignation. You don't have to ask anyone what those words mean, because I'm going to tell you. They mean anger, the kind of anger that comes from knowing that you're right and the other creature is wrong. I didn't know I had any righteous indignation in me, but when Blue flew Grand-mother's comb out of reach, the only bramble in my mind led to an ending in which Blue did *not* get away with doing something wretched yet again.

Did you know rabbits could climb? It's hard, but we can, especially when we're young. If you want to see for yourself, put a loose-linked wire cage around your blackberries. I dare you.

"Goosegrass," I commanded, "go straight back to the burrow. If someone notices I'm missing, tell them I'm visiting the cousins. I'm going to get the comb back."

"You?" Goosegrass looked up. "It's so high."

"I can do it quickly if you cover for me."

Goosegrass opened her mouth as if to protest but closed it again. "I believe you can," she said. "I'll see you in the burrow." With a nod, she turned and disappeared into the opening.

Even though she bungles nearly everything, you can see why I love my sister.

My righteous indignation transported me to the trellis. I hopped on, my hind paws on one slat and my front paws clutching the slat above. Swiftly I hopped to the second rung. The third.

On the third rung, my indignation left me.

My brambles began to unfurl like spiny fiddle-heads as I took in what I was doing. *What if Blue returns and pecks my exposed back? What if I slip and plummet to the ground and smash every one of my bones? What if an early-to-rise owl mistakes me for a snatchable snack?*

I'd been a fool to think that I, Butternut, had the mettle to pull off such a dangerous undertaking.

I got three rungs high and turned around was just about the worst story any rabbit in our colony had ever told, but it would have to be my story. I was about to hop down when a voice called out to me.

"I feel you, trellis trespasser! Are you friend or foe?"

My head snapped up. The voice was small and faint, as if muted by dandelion fuzz. It came from the crossbars.

"Who's there?" I asked. Above me, I could see only the robins' nest.

"A creature fervent for friendship and petrified of predators."

I was utterly confused. "Unless you're a banana, I'm not a predator."

"Terrific! I am not a banana. Piper Nofledge, at your service."

Nofledge. Was that like Firstfledge? "Are you a robin?" I asked. "Do you think you could knock that gold comb down to me?"

"Alas, my unidentified, banana-loving friend, I am confined to my nest. You shall have to continue the climb."

"I'm a rabbit," I told the voice. "I don't think I can do it."

"But you must! I am most eager to meet you. How high are you hovering?"

"Three rungs."

"And are the rungs farther apart as you go higher?"

"No."

"Are the upper rungs brimming with burrs? Or vexing vines? Or sticky sap?"

"No. It's the same all the way up."

"Well, there you go. If you've climbed three, you can climb them all, yes?"

The voice had a point. I took a breath. *Don't think,* I ordered myself, and hopped onto the next rung. I kept going. I didn't look down. I tried to be steady and quick. My body quaked nonetheless.

The voice whispered encouragements. "Not long now! Keep climbing! You must be a remarkable rabbit!"

At last, digging my claws into a crossbar, I wriggled my hindquarters over the top—rather ungracefully, if I'm being honest. I panted. There it was, Grandmother's comb, right next to me.

I'd made it.

"Hello, friend! You are magnificent and mighty! And bigger than I expected. In case you are hungry, may I reiterate that I am not a banana?"

Two scraggle-feathered baby robins were fast asleep in the nest of woven branches and fuzz. One scraggle-feathered baby robin was awake and looking at me. Its back was brownish gray and speckled, its eyes bright.

"Piper, was it? I'm not magnificent," I said, still breathing hard, "and I'd never eat a bird."

"A reassuring reality. May I ask your name?"

It seems silly now, but I hesitated. I'd had my day's fill of interactions with other species. Even talking with this nestling felt like another betrayal of our colony and of Grandmother's rules. But it was Piper's encouragement that had helped me keep my mind clear and bramble-free enough to reach the top of the trellis. I couldn't be rude. "I'm Butternut. It's nice to meet you."

"Likewise. And what, Butternut, brings you to the top of the trellis?"

I took a breath and told the story of the two squirrels and their stuck tails, of Goosegrass fetching the colony's most valuable comb to untangle them, and of Blue stealing it.

Piper listened with his beak resting on the nest's edge. "I haven't been alive long," he said when I finished, "but that was the most sensational story I've ever heard. I felt as if I were there with you."

For a moment his words pleased me so much I could think of nothing to say. I realized that this was the first time I'd told a story to a creature other than

a rabbit. "The rabbits in Milkweed Meadow are good storytellers," I said at last. "We practice a lot."

"You must be one of the best."

I didn't know about that. Grandmother Sage did save some of her highest compliments for me when we gathered in the root room. Mother often put me first in the lineup too. It's funny—I'm nervous about most things, but I don't have trouble sharing stories. Maybe it's because I don't spend time thinking about who's listening. When characters start doing things in my head and I find words that bring them to life in a way that feels true . . . well, I like that feeling better than any other.

"I didn't know you'd hatched," I said to Piper to change the subject.

"Mother and Father haven't told many creatures. Apparently that jay, Blue, the one who confiscated the comb? He embezzled an egg. They're striving to keep us safe. Me and my sister, Windy." He pointed a beak at one of the sleeping birds, then the other. "And my brother, Beaker."

I nodded. "We all know what Blue did. You must be so sad."

Piper twitched his head back and forth. "Yes and no. I never met the bird that egg would have hatched into. My mother says that sad and sorrowful things happen in Milkweed Meadow, as they do every-where."

"Blue is a menace."

"Well, he's just one bird. The meadow is chock-full of creatures, yes? We can cope with him."

I looked at Piper doubtfully. "You'll see, once you're out of the nest."

"That reminds me!" he chirped. "Will you watch me fledge, brave Butternut? My parents say in three or four days we'll be ready. I'm so hoping I'll be Piper Firstfledge! Secondfledge would be fine too . . . as long as I'm not Thirdfledge. It would be terribly torturous to be the last one out, don't you think? Secondfledges and Firstfledges mate with each other, but Thirdfledges are stuck having to find Thirdfledges. I will try my best—although if I prevail, the Thirdfledge name seems a forlorn fate with which to burden my brother or sister."

"You get your name based on the order you fly out of the nest?"

"Yes. I can't wait. Flying means freedom. Finding my own food, gliding on billowing breezes, finally meeting all the meadow-dwellers. And to think, I've already made my first friend!"

It was clear he meant me. I smiled. He'd soon learn the way everyone kept to themselves in Milkweed Meadow. Still I'll admit I was curious to see him fledge. Now that he'd built it up.

"If you fledge around dawn or dusk, I'll see you when I'm feeding," I told him. "And speaking of flying, I should get going. I wish I could fly off this trellis. Going down with the comb in my mouth is going to be harder than going up."

"Don't climb with it. Drop it down first."

The robin was young, but he had good sense. I batted it with my paw onto the lawn, where it landed with a light thump. "Good luck fledging, Piper."

"Farewell, brave Butternut!"

I thought of telling him that the name really didn't suit me. My brambling fears made me one of the biggest cowards in the colony—if not *the* biggest. The sound of it was nice to hear though, even for a minuscule moment.

Listen to that. I was starting to sound like him.

Climbing down the trellis was awkward, and I do not wish to dwell on it. I use the term *climb* loosely. It was more of a scramble and fall. But I landed on my bottom and no bones broke, I'm happy to say.

"Are you scraped, scratched, or squashed?" Piper called softly when I reached the ground.

"I'm okay."

"I look forward to my next story, fearless friend!"

Triumphant, I picked up the comb in my teeth and hopped home.

VI.

Mother, Grandmother, and Goosegrass were waiting for me in the entrance tunnel.

Usually the burrow was bustling at this time of night, my brothers and sisters tumbling around and chasing each other before bedtime. Tonight it was silent. I could see no one but the three rabbits facing me with solemn expressions. I imagined the rest of my family, just out of sight in the tunnels, straining to hear every word of the confrontation.

Trying to begin on an upbeat note, I lay the comb on the ground. "Your comb, Grandmother. I've brought it back."

It was unclear just how good Grandmother Sage's eyesight was. She wasn't completely blind, but she'd told us that age took a toll on rabbits' eyes. As a result she never seemed to look right at us. Her gaze meant a piercing study of our foreheads, noses, and ears. It wasn't comfortable.

She placed an arthritic paw on the comb. "No object is worth your life, granddaughter."

"I know," I said, "but I wasn't harmed."

"You were lucky," said my mother. "It's a miracle you didn't wind up in a hawk's belly. Goosegrass too. You ought to have returned to the burrow as soon as the squirrels appeared."

My sister stared at her paws. Sheesh, she'd had one task—to cover for me. How easy had it been to get the entire story out of her?

"Our milkweed is our smarts. Remember, kit?" said Grandmother Sage.

I remembered. But my heart was still thumping with the glory of having climbed an entire trellis. "I did something I didn't think I could do tonight—"

"We're not going to hear any more about it," my mother interjected.

"Gently, Nettle," said Grandmother Sage. "Butternut, what you will not do this evening is hold your sisters and brothers in rapture as you describe your adventure. Some stories are unspeakable because of the horrors they contain."

My mind immediately leaped to the mysterious coyote affair during Grandmother's journey to Milkweed Meadow.

"Stories that encourage disobedience are equally dangerous," she continued. "My job is to keep the colony safe, not have ideas planted in young rabbits' heads. You and Goosegrass will go to bed, and you will not speak of today's events, no matter how much your brothers and sisters pester you. Understood?"

I'd saved the hides of two squirrels. I'd performed a feat of athleticism. I'd met a young robin that spoke like an old poet. I'd not let Blue get away with mischief. I'd been brave.

And I couldn't say a word about any of it.

I don't know if there was some residue of righteous indignation in my head, but in that moment it didn't seem quite fair that there were certain truths we couldn't tell. I knew Grandmother wanted to protect us, but was silencing my story the way to go about it? Truth was truth, wasn't it?

"If you tell this story," said my mother, "you will be forbidden from telling or listening to any more stories in the root room."

Mother knew she had me then. A thorny bramble, in which I wasn't part of our family's tradition of storytelling, grew in my mind. It was more disturbing than brambles in which the burrow flooded or bugs ate the meadow. I couldn't imagine excusing myself and missing all those great stories. Never telling any more of my own. "Understood," I said.

"Understood," Goosegrass muttered.

"Another thing," said my grandmother. "You two are prohibited from participating in the next road test."

My mother frowned. "But—"

"They have had altogether too much excitement. They need to recover so their hearts and muscles are strong. I'm sure you agree."

Goosegrass and I shared a quick glance. I didn't know what she was thinking, but to me it felt like sweet relief not to have to cross the road in the next test, which Mother had scheduled in a couple of days' time. I wondered if Grandmother knew how much I was dreading my test. If this was a little gesture of kindness. I *had* brought her favorite comb back, after all.

"Fine," said my mother. "Now off to sleep with you both. Know that you have disappointed me, and I expect better behavior going forward."

"Sorry," whispered Goosegrass on our way to the slumber nest. "Mother took one look at me and knew something was up. If it's any consolation, my story came out pretty jumbled."

"I wish I could tell you what happened after you left."

"I wish I could hear it."

My brothers and sisters attacked us in the slumber nest, nipping our ears and batting our tails to get the story out of us. But neither Goosegrass nor I said a word. Finally Kale told everyone to leave us alone. Even Baby Sweetcorn gradually lost interest in hopping on my back and squeaking, "You climbed the trellis, didn't you? That's what Goosegrass told Mother. I think. Unless she said you hurt your pelvis. Or made some creature jealous? Tell, Butternut, tell!"

Eventually she settled down too.

Goosegrass and I nestled in a corner. She looked miserable, so I gave her a small smile. I couldn't be upset, not with Piper's small voice still in my head, calling me a "fearless friend."

The following day I peered up at the robins' nest while grazing. I couldn't see or hear the nestlings, and I wasn't going to get myself in more trouble by calling out to Piper. For now it was enough knowing he was there. For the first time ever, I had a secret. A sly, stealthy secret, as he would say.

The day after that, my brothers Watercress and Mallow and my sisters Clover and Thistle stood near the edge of the road with Mother. Kale, who had been first to pass his road test, waited to welcome everyone on the other side. The rest of us watched from the lawn.

It was late afternoon, our shadows long. I'd been hungry when we'd emerged from the burrow. We staggered the groups—rabbits in a clump are easy hunting, and a marching line would attract human attention. Well, can you imagine?

Before I could take a bite of grass, a vehicle rushed past, white and shiny and growling like a predator.

My hunger left me. It wasn't even my turn to take the test, and I had a cold stone filling my stomach.

Next we all had to dash for cover when a human-and-dog pair passed by on the sidewalk. The houses were spaced widely apart on the long road that ran adjacent to Milkweed Meadow. Still, dry weather produced a slow trickle of humans out for strolls, many with tethered dogs. If this dog decided to chase one of my family members, it could likely pull the strap out of the human's hand. So it was up to us to hide ourselves.

I waited in the brush at the meadow's edge with Chicory.

"An eventful start!" he said quietly.

I could hardly breathe for fear. When the dog passed, we emerged. I wondered how the test-takers were feeling.

Watercress was standing by the road's edge. He looked right and left and stood still a moment. From his stiff ears, I knew he was listening hard. Then he dashed across the pavement. Kale greeted him on the other side, and they hopped in celebration.

We chittered and clucked our approval.

Clover set off as confidently as Watercress had.

She was almost to the other side when something white fell out of the sky and landed on her face.

By this point in my story, you can guess the culprit. Which flying member of Milkweed Meadow caused trouble for no reason at all?

"Direct hit!" cawed Blue. He glided in circles above the road.

Clover tried to shake the droppings off her head. She continued crossing, although her path veered to the right. I wondered if she could see. When she reached the other side, she headed for a patch of grass and rubbed her face in it.

Poor Clover. At least she'd still passed. Safely.

"Hoppity hop! Hoppity hop! Why did the rabbits cross the road?" Blue taunted as he circled. "To prove that they're the snootiest creatures in Milkweed Meadow, is my opinion! That they're cleverer than the rest of us! That their droppings taste like rose hips!"

Mallow was up. He looked uncertainly at Mother. "You must learn to cross amid distraction," I heard her say. "Focus on the vehicles and ignore Blue. He doesn't matter."

Mallow tried to look and listen. Blue descended and began to bound over him, back and forth, as he started across. The bird shouted horrible things. How humans wanted to chop off Mallow's paws and attach them to chains for luck. How humans would someday

43

trap our whole colony and skin us all to make a coat. How we'd end up in a delicious stew.

I couldn't stop trembling. It was as if Blue were speaking my mind's brambles aloud. And inventing new and scarier possibilities.

When my time came, I would not, could not cross the road if that bird was taunting me.

Yet somehow Mallow made it. Blue flew over two passing vehicles to return to our side of the road.

It was Thistle's turn last. She was made of tough stuff. She never backed down in a quarrel. If anyone could tune out Blue's abuse, she could.

But she never got the chance. As soon as she hopped into the road, a high-pitched, piercing wail muted Blue's chatter—and everything else. I'd heard the wild sound only in my most nightmarish brambles.

It was the howl of a coyote.

Mother's head whipped toward the meadow, where a shadowy figure passed through the long grasses.

"Stay alive!" Mother hissed. "Back to the burrow! Kale, Watercress, Clover, Mallow, cross carefully!"

Blue took off into the tree canopy. The rest of us hopped as fast as we could across the lawn. I saw Goosegrass ahead of me. Chicory was on my left. We shot through the burrow's entrance tunnel and headed straight for the root room, knowing Mother would want to account for us all.

"Grandmother's unspeakable story," whispered Lavender. Her nose twitched like a dancing honeybee. No one said anything more.

Together, we waited. At last, wide-eyed and panting, Watercress, Clover, Kale, and Mallow entered the root room. Mother followed.

Quickly she scanned the room. Counting daughters, counting sons. "I believe," she announced, "we have all returned safely. And I believe our test-takers deserve a cheer. They used their milkweed today, that's for certain."

After a collective exhale, we chittered and clucked and nosed the triumphant rabbits. "Hen's teeth!" huffed Thistle. "I can't *believe* I didn't get a chance to cross. That Blue should just try to mess with me. He should just try it!" But under Mother's eye, she congratulated Watercress, Clover, and Mallow graciously.

Grandmother entered, her dragonfly comb between her teeth. She laid it down on the earthen floor. "I heard the howl. Oh, my dears. Thank goodness you're all here, safe and sound. Coyotes are capable of unspeakable horrors."

"Grandmother," Watercress said tentatively, "could you tell us anything more about what happened on the night you came to Milkweed Meadow?"

"We do *not* discuss it," Grandmother Sage replied. "Whatever you are imagining, the true story is far worse, gorier, and more gruesome. Listen to your elders, use your milkweed, and we can put an end to tragic stories in this colony. Now," she went on, "I sense that one of my grandchildren needs some grooming." Grandmother may not have been able to see the white splotches on Clover's face, but she could smell them. She began to clean Clover herself. "Would anyone be good enough to tell me the story of today's road test?"

Watercress began. The rest of us settled in to listen.

In the safety of the root room, the tendrils of my brother's story cradling and soothing us, the coyote seemed distant. But its howl hadn't felt distant out there on the lawn. It had felt dangerously close.

I remembered what Piper's mother had told him. *Sad and sorrowful things happen in Milkweed Meadow, as they do everywhere.* We could celebrate tonight and pay the howl no mind. But that didn't make it go away.

I wondered why the creature had howled. Had the dog startled it? Was it angry? Was it—calling to other coyotes?

Blue was bad, but some things, for rabbits, were worse.

VII.

I know you haven't forgotten about the rescue. I haven't either. It will make a humdinger of a climax—at least that's my hope. But first you need to understand the way the meadow began to change around this time. Connections began to form between creatures, thanks in large part to a single bird with an irrepressible spirit.

Here's another one of my favorite stories. It happened five days after I climbed the trellis and retrieved Grandmother Sage's comb. Blue didn't ruin things. Nor did a coyote. Some days call for uplifting stories without a whole lot of wickedness. I'm sure you'll agree.

Lessons got underway in the root room after breakfast. Mother was in the midst of her choking vines lecture, and we had just learned that the humans in the house were constantly cutting back the honeysuckle and buckthorn because of the damage they did to other plants. If we wanted to eat these delicious species, we needed to get while the getting was good. She had brought in blossoms for visual aids.

Suddenly a bright voice echoed inside the burrow and stopped Mother cold. "Good morning! Is Butternut in there? Brave Butternut the rabbit?"

Every eye turned toward me. Mother's mouth fell open, the honeysuckle blossom falling with it.

It wasn't Piper's voice, but it had something to do with him, all right. I waited for Kale to smirk and say something like, "*Brave* Butternut? That creature must be mistaken." But he didn't, and no one else did either.

"Stay here," said Mother. She hopped toward the entrance tunnel. Fortunately the burrow's hollow network carried the conversation to us.

"This is Mother Nettle. Please identify yourself."

"Mother Nettle, I'm sorry to bother you. This is Mother Firstfledge. My hatchlings tell me they feel ready to fledge this morning. One of my hatchlings, Piper, refuses to take the leap if your daughter, Butternut, isn't there to see him. Do you mind sending her out for a while? He's being rather stubborn."

A warm feeling spread from my ears to my haunches. Piper was waiting for me! I wondered if he would be Piper Firstfledge, Secondfledge, or Thirdfledge. I'd know soon.

48

Mother paused. "My kits are in the middle of their morning lessons."

I charged toward the entrance with a squeal. "Hang on, Mother Firstfledge!" I shouted. "*Mother*," I begged. "Please. I've never seen a bird fledge. Don't you think it could be educational? It's safe out there at this time of the morning. *Please*. I'll just watch them fly and come back inside. What's the harm? I'll—I'll even take my road test next. Please?"

Mother regarded me.

"Hurry," called Mother Firstfledge. "My babies are getting restless."

Mother let out a sigh. "The Firstfledges are a nice family. *For egg-layers*," she added in a whisper that I hoped stayed in the confines of the burrow. "All right. But your brothers and sisters come too."

I nuzzled her nose and hopped outside. Mother Firstfledge smiled at me before flying up to the crossbars. Soon my siblings had gathered on the lawn. Even Kale, looking dubious, was there. Together we squinted up at the nest. All I could see were some feathers shifting about.

"You met one of the robin babies!" whispered Goosegrass. "Incredible!"

I nodded without taking my eyes off the nest. Piper was in there. Piper was about to fly for the first time ever.

49

The other inhabitants of the meadow seemed to pause in their morning routines. The squirrels stopped collecting nuts and stared. The birds cocked their smooth heads toward the nest. I'd like to think that even Blue was perched somewhere, watching, quietly understanding what a solemn occasion this was. He'd fledged one day himself, after all.

I imagined that it took courage to jump off a nest and trust that your wings would keep you alight. But Piper had that kind of courageousness. He was the brave one, not I.

The three young robins appeared. They grabbed the edge of the nest with their claws, teetering a bit. I recognized Piper on the left. His feathers had filled in since I'd last seen him.

"Attention, all!" he called as loudly as his little voice would let him. "We are . . . Piper!"

"Windy!" said the middle bird.

"And Beaker!" said the bird on the right.

"*Firstfledge!*" The three birds hurled themselves into the air at exactly the same time.

Windy *flap-flapped* effortfully and flew all the way to the high branch of an oak.

Beaker made it to a limb on the feeder tree.

Piper rose into the air—but seemed to flap his wings too fast and at the wrong angle to catch the wind. In the next moment, he came crashing down on one of the house's glass skylights with a thud.

Head over tail, he rolled down the roof and landed in the rain gutter.

"Piper!" I called. Mother and Father Firstfledge hovered above him, nosing him with their beaks and chirping anxiously.

The creatures of Milkweed Meadow held their breaths.

Then—a snuffle. A faint chirp. Movement.

"Why is everybody so still and silent?" I heard. "I fledged! I flew! Brave Butternut, did you see me?"

I chittered and clucked and cheered, along with my brothers and sisters. And Mother and Father Firstfledge. And the other birds. And the squirrels. Even my mother, I noticed, was smiling in relief.

Piper's second flight, from the gutter to the ground, was much more controlled. He landed gently and hopped over to me.

"You did it! You're Piper Firstfledge!" I exclaimed.

"I am! Our rendezvous got me ruminating. Why should any of my siblings suffer the Thirdfledge name? A crumb of collective action, and we're all winners."

"Congratulations, Piper. I'm glad you made it out of the nest. *Now I don't have to climb the trellis to see you*," I whispered.

"Indeed. And I can drop down to hear one of your sensational stories anytime I wish! Now who are these fine furry folks? Introductions, if you please!"

I introduced Piper to my mother and to my five sisters and four brothers. He bowed his small head and talked to each one of them. He even gave some of them nicknames. Gallant Goosegrass. Thrilling Thistle. Bouncing Baby Sweetcorn. (That one he whispered to me privately.)

Then he wanted to meet all the other birds and squirrels. It began awkwardly—I'd been around the birds but had never bothered to learn many of their names because of Mother and Grandmother's lectures on keeping to ourselves for safety. But Piper's eager spirit charmed them all. I learned that the chickadee brothers were Pete, Skeet, Fleet, and Carlos. The woodpeckers were Vincent and Anjali. We met the cardinals, Tori and Efron, and the house sparrows, Amelia, Iris, and Toula, who assured us that their cousins would be around later. Culver the mourning dove I knew, but we met his extended family too. I was glad he didn't migrate after Blue picked on him.

Of course, I did know two of the squirrels, Inka and Twain, who bounded right over when I called. Their tails still looked wispy, but they didn't seem to mind.

"Butternut saved us," they chirruped. "Goosegrass too. They're brave and true. It's nice to meet you!"

"*Brave* and *true*, accurate adjectives," said Piper. "I knew Butternut was brave as soon as she traversed the trellis."

My sisters and brothers chittered. Kale gaped at me. I risked a glance at Mother, who was no longer smiling. "Butternut! Kits! It's time to complete our lessons," she announced. "Into the burrow. Now."

"Oh!" said Piper. "When will I see you again?"

"I'll be out for dinner," I replied. "At dusk."

"Dinner at dusk. Delightful. In the meantime, squirrels, would you introduce me to the rest of your frisky family?"

"Bye, Piper Firstfledge," I said shyly. "Congratulations, again."

"Farewell, first and finest friend!" With a little bow, Piper flew off, following the squirrels.

I filed into the burrow with my brothers and sisters. "So you *did* climb the trellis!" squeaked Baby Sweetcorn.

"Butternut." From behind, my mother bumped Baby Sweetcorn along with her head and hopped beside me. "Remember. No discussion of your antics."

"No, Mother."

"You saw the fledging. Therefore you will take your road test with Thistle and Goosegrass in the next round."

The road test. I'd promised that, hadn't I. My paws suddenly felt heavy. "Yes, Mother."

"This Piper character has certainly taken a liking to you."

I didn't know what to say. "He's nice."

"He seems nice, but you don't know him well. Be careful."

"Mother?"

"It is exciting to have a friend. But your first loyalty is to your brothers and sisters and the colony. Our rules keep us all safe. In other colonies rabbits don't receive education and don't look out for one another. Do you know what the average life span of those rabbits is?"

I waited.

"One year. One set of seasons. Rabbits that climb trellises and go frolicking with birds don't get to see another spring. Do you understand me?"

An unspeakable bramble coiled forth. *What if, next spring, Piper tells me about a delicious crop of crocuses, and on his encouragement, I recklessly wander away from the lawn to find them? What if a snake is waiting in the meadow, famished after its winter dormancy? What if its open mouth and fangs are the last things I see?*

Mother must have seen the worry in my face. "I'm not forbidding you from being friends with Piper. But remember your dignity. Use your milkweed. Stay alive. Understood?"

"Understood."

I told you this was a story without wickedness, so I probably shouldn't have included the snake. But it was only in my head, after all. And I'm not finished yet.

VIII.

True to his word, Piper found me when I emerged from the burrow at dinnertime. More accurately, he glided in three giant circles before landing. "I am showing off, Butternut! Flying is as fabulous as it looks. I have perused the entire property. Milkweed Meadow is filled with succulent bugs and cordial creatures. No glimpse of that glutton Blue, however. How are you?"

"A little jealous," I said. "You're making me wish I could fly."

"Ah, but you have an endowment that *I* envy. Would you tell me a story?"

I stared at him. He wanted a story. Now, at dinnertime, outside the burrow. After I got over my surprise, I felt honored that he'd asked. But I could feel my mother's eye upon me. I knew Grandmother would say that storytelling created connections between *rabbits* and made us a stronger colony. But neither she nor Mother had ever said that it was wrong to share our truths with other creatures. Not directly, anyway.

I decided that I could be Piper's friend and maintain my dignity. "I'll tell you one after I eat. This is my time to feed. Plus, I think better on a full stomach."

Piper was undeterred. "Swell!" He left me to eat and chattered in a nearby tree with Windy and Beaker.

The talking-to I thought might come from Mother didn't. She lingered within earshot but remained silent.

I suppose it was the desire to find inspiration for my story that made me look up. I froze as I spotted the little female human. Usually all the humans were on the first floor of the house at this time of day, preparing and eating a dinner of their own. But there she was, clearly visible through a window on the upper level, right above the grazing lawn. I looked around; none of the other rabbits appeared to have noticed her. She sat sideways, knees pointing up, cozily framed by the window glass. The outer pane was raised a tiny bit. That meant . . . the window was open.

But she wasn't looking at us. I peered closer. She was resting something flat on her raised knees

and held a stick-shaped object in her fingers. She was moving the stick around on the flat surface intently.

Grandmother had told us about the stories she'd heard in the human house. Most of them were inscribed, on printed pages. Humans could therefore read the same stories again and again if they wished. Grandmother didn't think putting stories on pages was any better or worse than telling stories aloud— just different.

I wondered if that was what the little female human was doing now. Making a story of her own. I didn't know how I'd ever find out—or ever get to hear it. But in that moment, I felt a connection to her. Did she, too, know the feeling of finding words that felt like truth?

In the meantime Piper was waiting for his story. He'd heard me describe the true events of the squirrel detangling and trellis climb. Perhaps, this time, I should tell him one of the stories I'd been rehearsing in the root room.

As my belly filled, and as I secretly watched the little female human mark down whatever it was she was creating, I decided I didn't feel like telling a story I'd already told.

So when Piper finally tucked his feet under his body on the lawn and peered at me with keen eyes, I began a new story. I think I was the only creature aware that a human might be listening, but I continued nonetheless.

"Once, a rabbit yearned for the power of flight. This rabbit was the only one in her colony who wished to see beyond the meadow, to track rivers as they wound, to glimpse hills as they rose. Her elders laughed and told her not to desire that which was unnatural for rabbits. Her sisters and brothers laughed at her, too, as she fashioned crude wings out of fallen bird feathers and mud. Not surprisingly, she couldn't lift off the ground, even with a running start, even on the windiest days. Her family told her to remove the ugly wings and return to her burrow, but she wouldn't, so she slept outside. On clear nights she looked up at the granular star canopy with awe. It seemed as if everything miraculous existed above her, out of reach. Desperate, she left home and hopped to a granite cliff top. 'At least I will know the pleasure of flying for a single moment,' she thought, and cast herself headfirst off the edge."

As I was talking, the creatures in Milkweed Meadow focused their attention for the second time that day—this time, on me. My brothers and sisters chewed softly enough to listen. The squirrels held their nuts and stopped scampering. Many of the birds seated themselves on the ground like Piper. I didn't look up at the human; whether she heard me or not, she made no sound either.

I took a breath and continued.

"The rabbit plummeted. She left a trail of feathers in her wake as her wings crumbled away. 'Whee!' she screamed into the abyss. 'Flying is everything I dreamed it would be!' Faster and faster she hurtled toward the firm earth below. She pointed her nose into the fall and prepared for impact.

"The wind admired her pluck. Swiftly it sent a paw-shaped gust and caught the rabbit. The gust carried her through the air, over the land. It carried her around the world. The rabbit saw not just rivers but sprawling oceans. Not just hills but ice-capped mountain ranges. When she'd completed her journey, the wind whispered to a lightning bolt, which took aim and struck. The rabbit's body broke into fragments, and the wind secured these fragments in the heavens, arranging them into a rabbit shape. She became part of the star canopy she had once admired, looking down on the land until the end of time."

When I finished, quiet stretched over the lawn like a fog.

At last Piper said, "Tonight I won't be able to resist looking into the sky for the star rabbit. What a stirring story."

"Thank you." I was glad I'd taken the risk with the new story in front of such a large audience. It had come out the way I saw it in my head, so I felt lucky.

"I was breathless when the rabbit fell."

"Prolonging the tension is a little storytelling trick," I murmured. "You shouldn't know she'll be safe right away."

"It was sad and happy at the same time," said Goosegrass.

"All right," said my mother. "Finish up, kits."

I chanced a glance at the little female human as I headed back into the burrow. She was no longer hunched over her knees, moving her stick around. Her chin was raised and she was staring skyward out the window.

I felt the energy of Piper's first flight. And the power of my story. They had brought so many different kinds of creatures together.

It was a good morning and a good evening in Milkweed Meadow.

IX.

Now that this tale is well underway, you're probably thinking that it's going to be about my friendship with Piper. We meet on the lawn. He reports on his morning aerial excursions, I tell dinner stories, and around and around we go.

Mother would call that a *boring second act*.

Fortunately that's not what's coming next. Yes, the story is about Piper and the part we both played in the rescue. But our friendship includes someone else too. This means there's another character for *you* to meet. And characters are like bananas: if they're good, you can never have too many. I like to think that new characters represent new perspectives—and that their flaws remind us of our own.

To this end there's a newcomer I must introduce. And *she* I met for the first time when her hoof smashed through the root room ceiling that very night.

I was asleep, but the crash woke me. It woke all of us. The thud sent vibrations deep into the earth. For a sleep-addled moment, I wondered if my story for Piper had come true and one of the fragments from the rabbit in the heavens had fallen on Milkweed Meadow.

My brothers and sisters began creeping through the tunnels, sniffing and listening.

"Stay behind me," whispered Kale. He didn't have to worry; fear kept me in the back of the pack. Brambles bloomed in my mind, but to be left alone in the slumber nest was worse.

"What could it be, Butternut?" Goosegrass asked. "Do you think we're about to be in another unspeakable story?"

I couldn't respond.

A loud bawl froze us all—then sent us hopping toward the root room.

The black cloven hoof in the middle of our lecture hall looked like something mythical. It wobbled, and we heard the bawl again, followed by a bleat. The hoof tried to rise through the ceiling, but the web of roots imprisoned it. It tried again, and again, and finally jerked itself free.

The night air and the light mist of rain falling through the ceiling made the root room feel different—

wilder and more dangerous. Mother and Grand-mother appeared and tried to herd us into bed, but my brothers and sisters weren't having it. Some of them peered up through the hole in the ceiling.

I ran with the others to the entrance hole and hopped outside.

The hoof belonged to a whitetail deer. A fawn, judging by her size and the spots on her back. She had large ears, not unlike ours.

One of her front hooves bent to the side unnatu-rally. It was terrible to look at. The fawn snorted and blatted and whistled, her eyes wide with pain. I twitched my forepaw, imagining what a broken bone would feel like.

The screen door opened, and the two little humans from the house stepped outside. The smaller, female human looked as if she wanted to run right up to the fawn, but the older, male one held her hand. They lingered on the flat stones near the lawn.

The fawn stared at them. She didn't run.

"It's okay," the little female human whispered. "We'll help you."

A new sound, a high wheeze, came from the meadow. I caught the flash of a white tail in the dark-ness and could make out the shape of a massive doe.

"Come back inside." The mother human held open the door. "We're supposed to leave it alone. Its leg will heal naturally, most likely." She knelt and pointed toward the meadow. "Look. Its mother will take care of it."

The father human came outside as well. No one was staring at the clump of us rabbits near the burrow entrance. Still it was strange to linger this close to the human family and to two deer. We formed a triangle of unacquainted species, and I understood why Grandmother had created her lessons to protect us. The others stood imposingly, while we huddled near the earth. I fought the instinct to dash.

"Come," the human mother said again.

The little male human hopped onto his father's chest and was carried inside. The little female tugged on her mother's arm. "Its leg is hurt. Look at it."

"We'll call a wildlife rehabilitator when we get inside. But they're probably going to say the same thing. It's worse to chase and capture it, love. It's a wild animal."

"But—"

"Come."

The mother led her daughter back into the house. All four humans remained by the window, watching. The little female human's face held a colony's worth of sadness—so much so that I forgot my own fears. I wanted to tell her that I felt what she was feeling. That it was hard to watch the deer suffer and do nothing, even if your elders said that doing nothing was the right thing to do.

We all watched as the fawn hobbled on three legs toward her mother. They entered the forest, and the dark spaces between the trunks engulfed them. I figured I'd never see them again—which only proves that you never can tell where your own story will lead.

X.

"We're going to make sure that fawn is healing heartily. Right, Brave Butternut?"

The next morning I couldn't wait to tell the story of the fawn to Piper. I'd even dreamed up language to describe the hoof's invasion of the root room. I thought I could compare it to a haunted branch, standing on end and pounding out a spell on the dirt floor of our burrow.

But since he'd made friends with nearly every bird and squirrel in Milkweed Meadow, Piper had already heard the news.

Sometimes it is a little gift to discover that a listener already knows a story you intend to share. You get the chance to reflect on it together. You're nodding. I know you agree.

In this case, though, not getting to share my story—or the branch metaphor—deflated me a bit. That is, until Piper and I were able to discuss how it made us feel.

"You should have seen the strange angle of the fawn's leg," I told him. "It was bent sideways when it was supposed to stick straight up and down. I remember the pain in the fawn's voice. The sadness in the small humans' faces."

"What an awful accident," Piper concurred. "It reminds us that our bones are brittle. But never fear," he continued. "The fawn can't have gone far. I'll investigate after breakfast. She may be resting somewhere secret, but I'll find her!"

I took a mouthful of grass, wet with last night's rain. "Just what will you do when you find her?"

Piper looked at me as if I had no sense. "*We* will talk to her! All creatures crave company! We'll ask her if she needs anything. Cheer her up. Let her know she has friends in Milkweed Meadow."

Does she? I wondered. Grandmother Sage told us that deer often passed through the meadow in the fall and early winter when they were breeding. Grandmother respected deer. Humans told many stories about them too. Like rabbits they were graceful mammals capable of intelligent thought.

They were also covered with ticks and other bugs. So they weren't *quite* as special as rabbits, at least the ones in our colony.

Climbing the trellis on the lawn was one thing. Traipsing off into the woods to talk to a fawn with a broken leg required real bravery. The kind I didn't have.

"Even if I wanted to, I couldn't go," I murmured to Piper. "We have lessons all morning. We can't wander off. Even at mealtimes, I'd be missed if I were gone too long."

"Then we'll nip away at night. When you're supposed to be sleeping. No one will search for you then."

I thought of the dark woods. "That's the worst idea of all."

"Why?"

"Because I will certainly be eaten."

Piper laughed. "But I will be with you! No one would dare!"

I stared at my small friend. I thought of the talons of swooping owls. I thought of the chilling coyote howl we'd heard during the road test and the shadow in the meadow grasses. How did he expect to fend off predators? With his tiny beak and hollow bones?

And yet, somehow, his supreme confidence comforted me.

"We must go," Piper said. "It is our duty. Imagine it were you, lying in a leaf bed, leg bone broken. You would want to know some creatures cared. Correct?"

I wanted to say that he had me all wrong. That I was the most fearful and timid rabbit in my colony. That with the way my mind worked, every trunk in the forest at night would become a wolf, every twig a snake.

But saying these things out loud would make them true. There was a part of me that wanted to imagine that I could be brave. That I could tame my mind's brambles to help a hurt fawn.

I sighed. "Wait outside the burrow entrance. I'll join you when the others are asleep."

Piper smiled. "I will, fearless friend."

Before I recount our dark and perilous journey, let me quickly mention one more thing. It was that morning that Piper finally met Blue.

The little female human came out to fill the feeder, and we all scattered. She also brought a pile of blackberries and raspberries and left them by the forest's edge on something round, white, and flat. I think she meant them for the fawn, and although my mouth watered for them, I didn't touch them. I'm sorry to say that my brothers and sisters didn't show the same self-restraint. Kale told me that if we didn't eat them, the birds or squirrels would, and what a waste that would be. Goosegrass did a sort of hopping dance while she tried to stand by my side. "My mouth waters for them, Butternut!" she exclaimed, and ran off to join my siblings. Together they devoured every last berry.

As usual Blue hogged the freshly filled feeder. Batted his wings at any other bird that tried to come close. Stuffed his beak with seed.

Piper watched. Before I could stop him, he'd hopped right onto a branch of the feeder tree. "Good morning!" he piped. Some rabbits and birds turned at the sound of his voice. "You must be Blue. It's nice to meet you at long last. My name is Piper Firstfledge."

Blue spat out a sunflower seed shell. He glanced at Piper—and kept feeding.

"I believe you ate one of my brothers or sisters," Piper went on. I couldn't believe his boldness. "I'd like you to know I hold no grudge or grievance. I would still like to be your friend."

Blue's head snapped toward Piper. He seemed to be sizing up the young robin. "*Friend?*"

"Yes. We should be a family in Milkweed Meadow, don't you think? Every creature counts."

It was a magical moment, when I wondered if Piper's earnest words were going to soften Blue. He looked genuinely surprised. He even stopped feeding.

But the other birds had suffered far too much of his abuse in their lifetimes. "If we're a family, Blue is the horrible uncle nobody likes," Amelia the house sparrow twittered.

"Yeah," said Skeet the chickadee. "The only creature Blue counts is himself."

The jay narrowed his eyes at their insults. "Too many *Firstfledges* in this stinking meadow," he said. "Too many *Firstfledges* who need to stop their chirping, is my opinion."

Blue flew to Piper's branch and, quick as a peck, closed his beak around Piper's beak. He clamped it while we all watched breathlessly. Piper didn't flinch.

Finally Blue released him. "I can make you stop talking, you know. Birds with crushed beaks can't eat. Don't make it."

"I know," said Piper. "I will stop speaking for now."

"Good."

If it had been me, I'd have raced away to the tree-tops, humiliated. But Piper just shook his head a few times and flew back down to the lawn.

"Are you okay?" I whispered.

"I am. That bird puzzles me so much."

"Puzzles you? He's a bully. Don't bother with him, or you'll end up with a broken beak."

Piper shook his head. "He could have broken my beak then. I'm not afraid of him."

"Everyone is." I told him about the way he'd tormented my brothers and sisters during their road test. How I wouldn't be able to pass mine with him squawking at me.

"He sounds miserable," said Piper. "But onward! We have an injured fawn to find. Wish me luck." He winked. "I shall see you tonight!"

XI.

So that I didn't lose my nerve, I told the cheeriest story I could in the root room that day. Chipmunks planned a party in a sunny spot in the meadow. They brought seeds and grains. Chipmunk decorators braided daisy chains and hung them about. Chipmunk singers sang. Chipmunk dancers danced. One shy little chipmunk wondered if he'd find a dance partner . . . and he did. Every chipmunk nearly burst with joy during the festivities.

It was sappy, but telling it made me feel good.

As I spoke, a spring wind came in through the hole the fawn's hoof had made. We had begun to repair it that morning with fresh dirt and twigs. It was Goosegrass, of all rabbits, who had had the idea to leave a tiny opening so we could feel fresh air and sunlight in the root room. To everyone's surprise, Mother accepted the suggestion. We planned to make a moss patch to seal the hole when it rained.

After the physical and mental labor of the day, my brothers and sisters fell asleep quickly. Sleep called to me as well, but I twitched my nose to stay awake. When I heard heavy breathing around me, I gingerly made my way over the slumbering rabbits and out of the burrow.

Piper flew down from the trellis and greeted me. "You made it! I know exactly where she is. Let's go."

And so, we went.

Have you been in the oak forest at night?

I imagine our experiences would be similar. At first shadows loom and mute all the colors, so it feels threatening. Then your eyes adjust, and you realize how much you *can* see. The leaf cover on the ground looks silver in the moonlight. The bark glistens. And your ears aren't as sharp as mine, but I bet you'd hear a good number of sounds, even so. The pattering as squirrels run in and out of their holes. The brazen song of crickets. The rubbery hops of a toad. The branches whispering to each other whenever the wind blows. If you ignore the creatures that can make a midnight snack out of you, then the forest at night is an enchanted setting for a story.

Unfortunately my brambles couldn't help but crowd my mind with images of lurking, hungry creatures.

But I'd made my choice. I managed my fear by making my way forward . . . extremely . . . slowly.

I drove Piper batty. "We will get to the fawn by morning at this rate."

"I'm trying to be cautious," I whispered.

"I will swoop and scratch at anything that attacks us," Piper said. "Besides, your delightful ears will hear danger coming. You don't hear anything now, do you? Most creatures are good-hearted. They want to persist peacefully."

I didn't share his faith. I was trying to use my milkweed. Hop by cautious hop, I wound my way through the tight growth. I retold myself the story about the happy chipmunk party and tried to imagine it was taking place somewhere in the forest.

Finally we came to a place where the groundcover was soft and the trunks grew thickly. I heard an animal's labored breathing.

Piper and I looked at each other. "She's just ahead," he whispered. "Behind the trees, in a little clearing."

"We don't want to startle her," I replied.

He nodded and chirped a few times softly. Then he whispered into the darkness: "Greetings, friend! We are two members of Milkweed Meadow, Piper the robin and Butternut the rabbit. May we approach?"

"We mean you no harm," I added.

The breathing quieted. There was no answer. Piper and I looked at each other again.

"We witnessed your accident," continued Piper. "Is there anything we can do to diminish your discomfort?"

More silence. "She might want to be left alone," I said.

"Poppycock," said Piper, and flew into the clearing. I scrambled through the trees after him.

The fawn was lying on the groundcover, her broken leg stretched out beside her on the grass. As we approached, she started to scrabble to her feet.

"Please don't move," I cried. "Rest your leg. It must hurt so much."

She examined us with glassy eyes. "What are you doing here?"

"We thought we might help you," said Piper.

The fawn snorted. "Can you fix my leg?"

"No," he admitted. "We cannot."

"Then you can't help." She winced as she resettled herself on the ground. "My beautiful leg. Ruined. Mother says it will heal like this. I will be misshapen forever."

"Will you be able to walk on it?" I asked.

The fawn let out a long sigh. "I don't know," she said glumly. "Even if I can, I'll have to stare at its ugliness. And so will everyone else."

Piper cleared his throat. "Sad and sorrowful things happen in Milkweed Meadow, as they do everywhere."

I didn't know how this was supposed to make the fawn feel better. "In case you didn't hear before, I'm Butternut," I said quickly. "And that's Piper. What is your name?"

The fawn sized us up. "I'm not sure I should tell you. You're strangers."

"That is precisely *why* you tell someone your name!" Piper exclaimed. "To go from being strangers to being friends."

Another pause. "I suppose. When you put it that way. I'm Winsome."

"Is your mother around, Winsome?" I asked, remembering the stately doe.

"She's nearby. Feeding." The fawn groaned as she repositioned her body. "My leg aches. Please go."

Piper and I glanced at each other. I knew he wasn't ready to give up. "Wounded Winsome, we offer you our friendship. We cannot fix your leg, but we can mend your spirits. Creatures shouldn't suffer in solitude."

It occurred to me how I could help. "I could tell you a story, if you'd like. To take your mind off the pain."

Piper let out a gasp. "Yes! Butternut's stories are blessings. They're filled with exciting escapades and characters you wish were real."

"No. Please." Winsome put her head on the ground and closed her eyes. "Please. Let me rest."

I tried not to take the rejection personally. She didn't know about the storytelling skills of rabbits, of course. It did seem unfair that Piper and I had risked our lives to visit her in the middle of the night and she didn't even offer up so much as a thank-you.

I shrugged at Piper. There seemed to be nothing else to do but leave.

He made one last attempt. "Now that we know where you're nestled, we'll visit again to see how you're feeling. Farewell, Winsome."

We were exiting the clearing when we heard her voice. "Carrots."

Piper turned. "Pardon?"

"Or apples. Or any kind of berries, really."

Winsome's eyes were open once again.

"My favorite foods. If you brought any of those when you came back . . . well, they would mend my spirits a little. If it isn't too much trouble."

"We will do our best!" said Piper. "Feel better, friend!"

"Thank you." She closed her eyes once more.

"Butternut," Piper whispered as we started back through the moonlit forest. "The fawn must be feverish. It's not harvest time. It's spring. How will we get her favorite foods this time of year?"

I knew.

XII.

The humans kept their garbage by the side of the house. Grandmother had braved the bins to find our combs and brushes. And once in a while my mother procured us some grapes or spinach as a special treat. As far as I knew, none of my brothers or sisters had ever explored the garbage bins.

But none of them had climbed the trellis or visited a fawn at night either.

"Follow me," I said.

We went slowly but perhaps not quite as slowly as before. The woods felt familiar. I led Piper back to the lawn and pointed at the bins with my nose.

"Aha!" he chirped. "Carrots or apples or berries . . . or *something* Winsome will want. Wise thinking, friend."

"Be careful," I whispered. "Grandmother told me that raccoons sometimes—"

A smash. One of the bins toppled over. Its lid flapped open, and a giant, furry creature began to sniff and devour the garbage. Her fur was dense and tinged a tawny gray, her nose pointed.

It wasn't a raccoon. It was a coyote.

The villainous creature from Grandmother Sage's unspeakable story was a short dash across the lawn from us.

If Piper or I had moved, the coyote would have spotted us. We could do nothing but stand like stones and watch as her mouth opened and closed, revealing long teeth. I tried not to blink. I tried not to twitch my whiskers. I hoped the stench of the garbage was enough to mask our scent.

Even Piper understood that this was not a creature with whom to make friends.

The coyote ate ravenously, and I figured something out as I watched her. She had a belly like the bellies I'd seen on some of my aunts. The kind that looked round and hard. The kind that swelled in size, little by little. The kind that needed extra feedings.

After she had eaten her fill, the coyote loped off into the darkness.

We waited in stillness and silence. At last Piper whispered, "Was that creature a coyote?"

"It was a *pregnant* coyote," I said. "There will be a

mother and a litter of coyote pups in Milkweed Meadow."

"I hope she didn't eat all of Winsome's favorite foods." Piper hopped a few steps toward the toppled bin. "Let's see what's left."

I didn't join him. I was quivering all over. Life-and-death stakes might enhance a story, but they were terrifying to live through. I was supposed to be asleep next to the furry bodies of my sisters and brothers, not stumbling upon the most ferocious creature in all of Milkweed Meadow. I was not an explorer or an adventurer. I was a phony.

"Piper." I spoke in as loud a whisper as I dared. "I cannot visit Winsome again. I cannot keep taking these risks with you. There is a hungry, pregnant coyote nearby. I must follow my colony's rules. I must stay alive."

I'll never forget the way Piper looked at me that night on the lawn. His cheerful face turned stern and serious.

"You are not safe," he said.

"I know that! Every day I list in my head the horrible things that could happen in Milkweed Meadow." I paused—it was hard to talk so openly about my brambles with someone other than Goosegrass. It wasn't exactly the kind of talk that endeared you to other creatures. But if Piper wanted to be friends with me, he needed to know the truth. "I'm not brave," I said. "I'm full of fear. I'm sorry if I led you to believe something different."

Piper approached and put his tiny claw gently on my paw. "Oh, Butternut. We're all full of fear. You rabbits make cautious choices, like eating in a herd twice a day—but what's to stop that coyote from catching you at a mealtime? Or an eagle from eating me? Or Blue from stealing another bird's egg? We can't ever make ourselves safe. I, for one, would rather take a chance to help a friend in the forest at night than follow some silly rules that may or may not protect me."

Silly rules? No one in the colony would dare call Grandmother's rules silly. Rabbits were silly when they *didn't* follow the rules.

My brambles were silly. Foolish. Fearful.

But . . . what if they weren't? What if my fears were reasonable possibilities? And the silly thing was thinking that following rules would guarantee my safety when I could never truly avoid danger?

What if rabbits couldn't actually make their own milkweed?

I rolled the thought around in my mind. It felt like a truth. A difficult one.

Piper didn't say anything more. He hopped to the bins and began to sift through the contents with his beak. After a moment he picked his head up and smiled.

"Sometimes taking chances brings treats and treasures."

I took a tentative step toward the bins. Then another. I craned my neck to see. The coyote had left us plenty.

We feasted on bread crusts, raisins, lettuce leaves—which Piper didn't care for much—and a giant pile of peanuts, which I avoided but whose shells Piper pecked his way through eagerly. In fact, he decided to hoard as many as he could in his old, abandoned nest. While he covered his treasures with leaves and mud, I polished off my best discovery of the night: a delicious brown banana.

We also found a whole carrot, only a little soft, which we rolled behind the bin to save for Winsome. We hid an apple core for her as well.

When we both had bellies almost as big as the coyote's, Piper looked at me. "You don't have to come tomorrow, Butternut," he said. "Your fears must be a burden. I don't want to force you to face them, friend."

By then I had made up my mind. "But if I don't go, only you will get to see the look on Winsome's face when she sees the carrot. That's not fair, is it?"

Piper smiled. "It is undoubtedly unjust."

"I'll meet you at the same time tomorrow night. I'd better get some sleep."

"You will always be Brave Butternut," said Piper. "But tonight, if I may say so, you are also a most resilient rabbit. Sleep well."

"G'night," I replied, and crept into the burrow. No one was waiting for me in the entrance tunnel. No one woke up when I snuck back to my corner of the slumber nest. I snuggled in next to Goosegrass and fell asleep thinking about my night in the forest and how visiting Winsome and evading the coyote were the most daring things I'd likely ever do.

Of course, I had no idea then that the rescue was still in my future.

XIII.

It's an odd thing, to have faced danger and to go on with your ordinary life.

I studied the faces of my brothers and sisters the next morning. Did I seem different to them? Bolder? Worldlier? Would Kale look at me with newfound respect?

No one treated me any differently. Well, Mallow gave me a shove when I drowsily trampled on his tail on the way to breakfast, but that was it. I should have been happy, I suppose. I hadn't drawn suspicion.

In order to keep my excursion a secret but still warn my colony, I decided to tell Mother and Grandmother that Piper had seen a coyote near the garbage bins at night. It wasn't a lie, not really. Mother stiffened. "Was he sure?" she asked. "He's a young robin."

I told her he was.

"A shame," said Grandmother. "I thought that one from the road test might have moved on. They stalk about in the dark, usually. Be sure to bring those kits in well before dusk, Nettle."

"I keep them safe," my mother replied. My whiskers twitched guiltily.

That night at bedtime, Kale told a story about a rabbit that fell into a well. "She cried out to her brother for help," he said as we nestled together, "so her brother lowered the water bucket. But when she climbed in, he found she was too heavy to pull up. He called another brother over—still, they couldn't raise the bucket. The brothers quickly fetched their entire colony to pull the rope with their claws and teeth. *'One, two, three!'* the first brother yelled. The twelve rabbits together heaved so hard that the bucket came flying up and clanged against the pulley, and the rabbit inside flew out like a comet. Fortunately she landed on a boxwood shrub and only had the wind knocked out of her. Her family fussed over her and dried her off and picked clover for her dinner. After that, she was always careful where she stepped."

I'd been jumpy about my second night visit, but Kale's story made me laugh and settled me down. It also reminded me of what Piper had said about a crumb of collective action having a big impact. Bringing treats to a hurt creature would have an impact too. After everyone was sleeping deeply, I crept out to meet my friend once again.

I carried the carrot through the forest in my teeth, and Piper rolled the apple core ahead of him with taps from his beak. I still hopped cautiously, but when I grew fearful, I didn't try to ignore my brambles. "Yes, Butternut," I told myself. "A badger could eat you. Or a snake. Or that coyote with bottomless hunger. It could all happen. But a creature could put its hoof through the slumber nest overnight and squash you too. Or a ferret could twist its way into the burrow. You aren't safe. So taking a carrot to Winsome is a better way to spend your night than dozing. Keep hopping."

I did. And we made it.

And was it worth it! We clucked to let Winsome know we were near and entered the clearing with our gifts. Her face lit up with surprise.

"Oh my! But how—? A carrot *and* an apple? I don't believe my eyes. You two are wonderful!"

We placed our gifts near her mouth, and she immediately took a big crunch of carrot. She closed her eyes with pleasure and chewed. My mouth watered a little as I watched her.

"Butternut knew where to find them," said Piper. "A coyote almost ate them, but we got lucky."

"A coyote!" Winsome's eyes widened. "Is it part of a pack?"

I thought of the howl during the road test. "We don't know. We didn't see any others."

"Oh, please, please don't let it find me before my leg heals."

I felt for the fawn. At least I could run for it. "How does your leg feel today?" I asked.

Winsome took a bite of the apple core. "Mmm," she said. "About the same. The pain is a constant thrum. I'm getting used to it. If I lie perfectly still, it's manageable. If I scratch an itch, it's terrible."

"Do you itch?" asked Piper. "I could eat some of the bugs on your back, if you liked."

"They're all yours," Winsome replied. "That would be lovely."

Piper hopped behind Winsome's neck and began pecking at her fur. I tried not to think about what he was picking off. The thought of eating insects made me want to rinse my mouth with stream water.

"And—er—I could tell you a story." I hesitated to make the offer because I didn't want to be turned down again. "Only if you're not in too much pain."

Winsome looked at me with curious eyes, the way Kale often did. As though she was trying to figure me out. Her lashes were so long, even on her lower lids. Suddenly I felt shy and wanted to tell her to forget about the story. But then she said:

"Mother says not to trust anyone but other deer. She says deer are the most elegant forest-dwellers.

We are strong and fast and proud. Of course, with my bum leg, I'll never be as elegant as she." She snorted, then winced from the pain. "I probably shouldn't tell you this, but Mother calls rabbits hopping moss clumps."

Piper picked up his head and looked at me.

Hopping moss clumps. What was I supposed to say to that?

"Obviously she's wrong," Winsome said quickly. "I will tell her it was a rabbit that thoughtfully brought me a carrot. And I would love to hear a story, Buttercup."

"It's Butternut."

"My apologies. Come closer so I can hear you."

I began. I figured since there were three of us, I should tell a story with three characters. So I told Winsome and Piper about three little field mice that shared a nest in the oak forest. One discovered a beautiful stone, a piece of white quartz that looked like ice that never melted. It was too heavy for the little mouse to carry back to the nest she shared with the others. She could have asked the other mice for help—but she didn't want to share the stone. She knew it was selfish of her, but she had grown attached to the sparkling object. She wanted to rub her paws on it and gaze at her blurry reflection on its facets.

"I'm moving to a different nest," she announced to the other mice.

"But why?" they asked. "We share food. We warm each other's bodies on winter nights. Life is harder alone."

"Perhaps," said the first mouse. "But if I don't live on my own, I will be unhappy."

The two mice tried to support the first mouse's wishes. They helped her find a new place for a nest. They helped her build it out of grass. They helped her stock it with food.

"We aren't far," they said. "Please visit! And we will visit you!"

"Wait a few days until I get settled," the first mouse told them.

She ran to her precious stone, where two blue jays were waiting. She had hired them to help her move it to her new home. At last she would be able to stare at it day and night. "You may fly it over now," she told them. "As I promised, I will give you a pile of acorns each."

But the jays had been inspecting the stone and felt its beauty was worth more than acorns. They each grabbed a side and flew it up to the thick tree canopy where they roosted.

The mouse was heartbroken. She returned to her new nest and felt lonely and sad, since she was missing both her stone and the company of the other mice. For two nights she slept badly. On the third day, she returned meekly to the two mice, who welcomed her back into their nest.

The first mouse figured she would never see the stone again, but to her great surprise, she found it one day on the forest floor. She didn't know whether a wind had knocked it out of the treetops or if one of the jays had discarded it. It was as beautiful as she remembered, but she was a different mouse than before. She had known loneliness.

She immediately brought the other mice over to see the stone. They touched its surface with their paws and stared at their reflections. "Shall we carry it home?" they asked.

"I think we should leave it here," said the first mouse. "It's pretty but it will crowd our nest."

"Good point," said the others, and they went about gathering food. They decorated their home with star-shaped phlox flowers in the summer and snuggled close together in the winter and lived happily.

I paused and then whispered, "The end."

Winsome had closed her eyes, and for a moment, I thought she was asleep. Then she sighed. "Oh, that was lovely. I could see everything in my head. Especially that pretty quartz stone." She opened her eyes. "Did you think all that up? Or did it really happen?"

"It didn't happen," I said. "I've seen field mice in Milkweed Meadow. There are quartz peastones along the path around the lawn. Ideas just come together in my head sometimes."

"I liked the ending," said Piper. "I'm glad the two

mice welcomed the other one back, even though she had left them."

"And what terrible thieves the jays were," said Winsome. "Mother dislikes blue jays. They squawk up a storm as we pass through the forest, telling the humans who hunt deer where we are. As do most birds. I'm sure you wouldn't though, Piper."

I was starting to think that Winsome's mother sounded even more outspoken than my own, calling rabbits *hopping moss clumps* (I would never forget *that* insult) and disparaging other species. Aloud, I said, "We have a mean jay in Milkweed Meadow named Blue."

"Tell me more about the meadow," Winsome said. "Mother likes to stay deep in the forest in the warm months. I saw the house lights glowing so beautifully and wanted to explore. It was foolish, of course. Now, here I am."

Piper and I told her about the bird and squirrel and rabbit families that lived there. We told her about Blue's egg theft, which seemed to confirm her feelings about blue jays. Piper told her about his fledging, and I told her about our colony's storytelling lessons. Piper described flying over and over the forest until he spotted her speckled coat in the clearing.

"You rabbits and robins are remarkable creatures!" said Winsome. "I am like the first little mouse in your story, Butternut. Grateful for your company."

Piper was loveably insufferable on the journey home. "I told you if we found Winsome she'd become our friend. I *told* you all creatures crave company. We were able to help her, and how! My belly is full of ticks. She savored your story. I'm raring for our next rendezvous!"

"Let's see how much we can carry next time," I said. "We could have a midnight picnic."

"Spectacular!"

Storytelling works up an appetite, after all. It should never be attempted on an empty stomach.

To that end, please excuse me while I nibble a few bites of grass.

XIV.

Delicious. Now back to it. Winsome's leg slowly began to heal. A few nights later, she showed us that she could run on her three good legs for a short distance without much pain. She bounded into the forest's depths and returned straightaway. "I couldn't outrun the coyote yet, but I don't feel as helpless," she told us, panting. "My other front leg has to work so hard though. Do I look gangly and hideous?"

We assured her she did not. "You are as nimble as a nuthatch," said Piper. "As lithe as a lark."

Deer are long-legged and rabbits are squat, but the way a deer runs is similar to the way a rabbit runs. Watch us, if you get a chance. We both make little arcs in the air, as our hind legs follow our front. I was too bashful to mention the similarity to Winsome or

Piper, but it interested me. I wondered if I could put it in a story.

"I found this tangled in some briar today," Winsome said, producing a glossy ribbon from under a pile of leaves in the clearing. She waved it in her mouth. "I thought it was a blue jay. Isn't it pretty?"

It was indeed the color of jay feathers, a startlingly bright blue.

Piper looked at it with interest. "Pretty *and* practical. That strand would be serviceable when it comes time to knock together my nest."

Winsome tilted her head and eyed the ribbon. "That's not for a while, right?" She tucked it under the leaves again. "I'll give it to you when the time comes. I promise."

On a subsequent visit, Winsome could put a little weight on her healing leg. We had brought two apple cores, and she munched hers from a standing position. The one I'd brought for myself had some kind of peanut spread on it that Piper was happily cleaning off for me.

We were playing I Spy, a guessing game Grandmother Sage had taught my brothers and sisters. Winsome kept spying "something lovely," which didn't help Piper and me much, since Winsome thought every tree, every blossom, every ray of moonlight, and every rock in the forest was lovely. Piper had correctly guessed the shiny trail of a snail making its way up a nearby trunk when I sensed we were being watched. I turned sharply to see the dark shape of a doe peering at us from the edge of the clearing.

"Oh, hello, Mother," said Winsome. "These are the creatures I told you about. Piper the robin and Butternut the rabbit. My friends."

The doe approached. Have you stood next to a full-grown doe or buck? I imagine you'd find one imposing. Now imagine you're my size! I was just getting used to Winsome, and her mother was broader and longer necked, with hilly muscles running up her legs and back. I did feel a little like a moss clump as she examined us.

Piper gave his usual chipper greeting. The doe looked at me. And then at my apple core. My doubts about milkweed may have been deepening these days, but Grandmother's lessons to *respect your elders* came immediately to mind. Even though this elder didn't have the highest opinion of my species, I wanted to show her that rabbits were well-bred animals. "It's nice to meet you," I said as loudly as I could muster. "Would you like this core? You're welcome to it."

She blew air through her nose in a snort. I don't think she did it on purpose, but a few droplets of mucus landed on the core.

"There is a fallen tree about eighty paces in the direction of the large beech," she said to Winsome.

"Full of good mushrooms." With that she walked off into the woods.

"Thank you, Mother!" called Winsome after her.

I was so curious. "Does your mother . . . spend time with you during the day?"

"She knows where I am," said Winsome. "She's teaching me to be independent. In the summer we'll join up with other does and fawns. Mother will want to lead the herd. If she's in charge, she can't watch over me every moment."

I had no doubt that Winsome's mother would lead her herd.

Winsome let out a soft sigh. "I can't be a burden." She didn't look at her leg, but I imagined she was thinking about it.

A day came when Winsome told us the thrumming of pain had changed to occasional tenderness. She was still bothered by the angular way the leg bone had healed. I tried to point out that between her lashes, her dark eyes, her shiny speckled coat, and her wink of a white tail, no one would take her for anything other than a beauty. I expected her to be pleased at the compliments.

"You're wrong," she snapped. "When everything else is normal, you notice the thing that isn't."

I wondered if her mother had made this comment to her. My feelings were hurt, but the sting didn't last. I considered how she must see herself—

and how she needed to know that she wasn't alone. "I know a little bit about not being like every other rabbit. I look like them. But my brothers and sisters are courageous, and I'm terrified most of the time."

"And yet here you are with us," Winsome said.

"Still, fears knot themselves in my mind like wild brambles and make everything harder."

I felt the light touch of Piper's wing feathers on the side of my body.

Winsome's face turned thoughtful. "Do your family members make fun of you?"

I considered. "That's the funny thing. I don't think they do, not really. I think the creature that disapproves of my brambles the most . . . is me."

"I see," Winsome murmured. She looked at her leg for a long time and then looked back at me. "You can't help your fears, and you're still a lovely friend. Don't be hard on yourself."

I hoped she heard her own truth in her words. "Thank you," I replied. "I'm trying."

We didn't visit Winsome every night, because the mornings after were painful for me. I shuffled sleepily to breakfast and, despite my night snacking, chewed as much grass as I could stuff into my mouth. Something about not sleeping made me ravenous. My eyes drooped during lessons. I was grateful to have so many brothers and sisters eager to answer Mother's questions.

One blessing: I was inspired to tell new stories in the root room. I shared the one about the mouse trio and the quartz stone. Grandmother winked and called it "a real gem." I told another about a herd of deer that outsmarts a wolf in the woods. And another about woodpeckers who open a scouting business to find lost animals in the forest. In my head they were robins, but I figured everyone would assume I was thinking about Piper. I didn't need Mother's eyes to narrow.

In fact, Mother loved my stories. "You are capturing deep truths, my daughter," she told me privately after one of our sessions in the root room. "The misery of a life apart from other creatures. The power of compassion. Your truths will guide your generation in the colony. I know you have fears inside you, but you have boundless wisdom as well." Her face remained serious, and she stared at me intently. "I see that in you."

It was the nicest thing Mother had ever said to me. I looked at the dirt floor and mumbled my thanks.

XV.

Before the rescue, something extraordinary happened one night in the forest.

I rode on Winsome's back.

You heard correctly. *I*, Butternut the rabbit, rode on the back of a deer.

And not just a little ride either. She curved around brush. She leaped over fallen trunks. And I didn't fall off!

It began when Piper and I found no sign of Winsome in the clearing one night. We whispered as loudly as we dared into the darkness. We frowned at each other. By now you know where my mind's brambles raced—to a certain hungry animal with a belly full of babies. What if Winsome had been chased? What if we never saw her again?

It was an unspeakable possibility.

"You wear your worry on your face, friend," said Piper. "Don't despair. I will scan the surroundings for her."

I nodded, and he flew into the treetops.

It won't do to draw out the tension here, because you know we found her. Let me simply say that while I crouched alone on the leaf cover, an owl passed over me. I had never seen an owl before, but I knew it from its pointed feather tufts and silent wingbeats. It glided overhead and didn't stop.

I did not like the way this night was starting out.

Then Piper returned, triumphant—he'd spied Winsome feeding on some flowering shrubs near the beech. When we approached, she apologized for having alarmed us. "I have an idea!" she said. "The next time I roam, I'll mark a trail for you." She stomped her uninjured front leg in the dirt. Three hoofprints formed a line. "You'll have to track the markings to find me!"

"We'll be forest scouts!" exclaimed Piper. "Let's play!"

I, too, imagined what a fun new game this would be—provided someone kept me company as I scouted.

"In a bit." A mischievous look crept over Winsome's face. "Piper, I've been thinking. How fast can you fly?"

Piper cocked his head to the side. "I'm reasonably rapid."

"Race?"

It took us both a moment to understand. "You want to race Piper?" I asked.

"I went for a gallop today, and I felt good! I don't know if I'm as fast as I used to be, but I *thought* I might be as speedy as a flying bird. Will you race? And fly your fastest, okay? Butternut, do you want to race too?"

I did not. And I wasn't thrilled about the two of them crashing through the forest. "I saw an owl tonight."

"Oh, an owl won't get you while I'm here. If you don't race, you can determine the winner."

They decided on the route and the rules. I waved my paw for the start. It was sort of thrilling to see them speed away. They curled around a distant oak and returned. I did wonder if Piper would let Winsome win so that she'd feel that her leg had healed well—that was the kind of bird he was. And Winsome did win. But when I saw how powerfully Piper flapped his wings back to our spot and how winded he was afterward, I decided she'd beaten him for real.

"I knew I was as fast as a bird!" Winsome declared.

"Faster," croaked Piper. "Much faster."

"Rematch?" She smiled.

"You will triumph time and time again," he panted. "It's not an even contest."

"Shall I give you a head start? Or . . ." The smile returned. "I know. What if I carry Butternut on my back?"

I was momentarily speechless.

His chest still heaving, Piper looked at me in delight.

"You should have a little fun too, Butternut. Come on." Winsome lowered herself onto her belly. "Trust me."

I made her promise not to dart away. To stay still until I made my pawholds secure. To start with a slow walk. To let me off if I'd had enough.

And then I climbed on. Wouldn't you have?

Animals kept as pets are transported from place to place in carriers. Humans ride in strollers and vehicles. Even some baby spiders spin draglines and balloon away on the wind. But I'd never had the feeling of moving from one place to another on anything but my own paws. Riding on Winsome's back, looking down on the forest floor, the breeze rustling my fur when she sped up, felt like magic.

To keep from falling, I threaded my claws into Winsome's speckled coat and gripped her back with my paw pads. She didn't let me sink my claws too sharply into her skin. I really did have to trust her. But I could feel her trying too—keeping her back as level as possible, slowing down after a jump so I could steady myself.

"Look at those birches," Winsome said as we passed through a small cluster. She sighed. "The way the moonlight makes their trunks gleam. Aren't they beautiful, Butternut? Don't you love this forest?"

We ended up not racing Piper; neither of us felt ready for a full-out sprint. But we went fast, believe me. Piper flew around excitedly and sometimes perched on Winsome's back with me.

"What a ride!" I shouted into the night air. I couldn't help myself!

When Winsome tired, I got off and thanked her. She brushed away the gratitude. "Anytime. What are friends for?"

We played forest scouts, and no one made me scout alone. After that I told a story. There was no sign of the owl again.

As I bade Piper farewell under the moonlight and headed toward my burrow's entrance, I thought of the way the fearsome night had turned into one of our best nights.

And it had—until something bolted out of the burrow right at me, and I yelped so loud it was a wonder all the owls in Milkweed Meadow didn't come diving.

XVI.

"I knew it! I *knew* you'd been sneaking out. Butter-nut, where *were* you?"

The something that had bolted from the burrow was my eldest brother, Kale. He paced back and forth outside the entrance and glared at me as I caught my breath.

"How—how did you know?" I panted.

"It wasn't hard. You've looked so tired during your lessons. And you're always whispering to that robin fledgling. Tonight, when I woke up and couldn't find you in the slumber nest, I waited here. So? *Where did you go?*"

I felt my body fill with heat. I thought I'd been so secretive. I should have known my eldest sibling was keeping an eye on me. Telling Kale the truth felt like ending something special and private. Then again, the truth was the only thing that made my sneaking out halfway forgivable. He was perceptive enough to see through a lie anyway.

"To the forest," I whispered. "With Piper. We've been visiting the fawn that hurt her leg in the root room. Her name is Winsome."

Kale stopped pacing. His words slowed in the way Mother's did when she was delivering an important part of a lesson. "Butternut. Have all of Grandmother's teachings meant nothing to you? It's up to us to avoid tragic stories in our colony, and here you are, *seeking out* tragedy in the forest." I had trouble holding his gaze, it was so full of judgment and disappointment. He came closer and peered at my back. "Look at you. In addition to putting everyone in danger, you're covered in ticks." He pulled a few off with his teeth and spat them away. I squeezed my eyes shut and tried not to think about the vermin crawling in my fur.

When he finished grooming me, he sighed. "I have half a mind to wake Mother to talk some sense into you."

"No!" I hopped around him and blocked the burrow entrance with my body. Mother would make sure I *never* went to the forest at night again, even if it meant sleeping in the entrance tunnel herself. "Listen to me. I think—I think that Grandmother's lessons might be wrong."

"Don't be absurd. Grandmother's lessons have protected three generations in this colony."

The conversation Piper and I had had by the garbage bins came back to me. "We rabbits are never fully safe, you know. No matter what Grandmother says. No matter how we behave."

Kale sounded as if he was trying to stay patient. "Maybe so, but it's senseless to take foolish risks."

"Visiting Winsome isn't a foolish risk. She was injured, and Piper and I cheered her up. We bring her food. I tell her stories. Helping a creature is a good reason to take a risk. Isn't that what so many of our stories tell us to do? To help others?"

"Well, those are just— Stories aren't the same as real life."

"Why not?"

Kale didn't answer me.

"Real life is where the truth in our stories should count most," I continued softly. "Isn't it?"

The perfectly groomed, perfectly brave, perfectly rule-following Kale looked at me in a way he'd never looked at me before. "Well . . ."

"Just think about it," I pleaded, "and don't tell Mother."

"Fine. I won't, for now. Is the fawn—is Winsome healing all right?"

I nuzzled his nose. "She's doing very well. Thank you, Kale."

He cleared his throat. "You'll need an extra thorough grooming tomorrow, though. See to that."

"I will."

I followed my brother back to the slumber nest. He watched me snuggle next to Goosegrass in my usual spot. Then he rolled over on his back and stared at the ceiling. He didn't close his eyes.

I couldn't sleep either. I poked Goosegrass until she woke up. "Mmm?" she mumbled.

"I snuck out of the burrow tonight and went to the forest," I said in my softest whisper. "And Kale caught me."

"That's nice. See you in the morning." Goosegrass's breathing deepened.

"Goosegrass!" I hissed. "Did you hear what I said?"

"Mmm. Snuck out to the forest," she murmured. Her eyelids fluttered and then opened. "Why, Butternut, have your brambles gone away? Are you not fearful anymore?"

"*Shh*. I'm petrified. But . . . it's fun. I'm with friends. And it's beautiful. So I go."

Goosegrass was waking up fully now. "Do you want to tell me the story?"

I glanced over at Kale. He could likely hear us, but if he did, he gave no sign. He was still staring into the air.

So I whispered the story of my night visits to Goosegrass. I half wondered if she'd ask to come the next time I went, but her eyes grew wide when I described the shadowy and ominous journey to Winsome's clearing. "You did *that* instead of sleeping?" was all she said.

The midnight storytelling proved too much for her, however. The next morning my tired sister fell fast asleep on the root room floor in the middle of a lesson on story symbols and motifs. Fortunately, as it was Goosegrass, Mother just sighed and carried on.

Later that same day, Piper and I went to the stream for a drink after lessons. I could feel Kale watching me as I made my way through the meadow, but thankfully, he didn't call out or try to stop me.

Three weeks had passed since I'd first met Piper. Mother told us that if her seasonal senses were correct, we had reached the year's longest days. The forest's dense, leafy canopies soaked up the bountiful sunlight. As we made our way, I told him the names of the different buds bursting into bloom: the pink, five-petaled flowers that grew low to the ground were spring beauties; the light blue ones on tall, hairy stems were chicory (my brother's namesake!); a few early daisies peered at the sun.

Whoops! I promised to keep the second act peppy, and here I go detailing the meadow's botanical changes. There's no need to yawn so dramatically. This is the longest story I've ever told, after all!

Back to action, then. It wasn't long before we spied Blue in a nearby tree—and he was not alone. There was another jay nearby, on a higher branch.

"If you stayed, I'd protect you," Blue was saying to her. "If someone bothered you, I'd pull out his wing feathers until nothing was left but pimply skin. Then I'd make him eat one of the feathers."

The jay made a face.

"You'd never go hungry. I eat first at the feeder, but you'd eat second. That's a promise. The meadow's full of brainless creatures, but we don't need to talk to anyone else. One of the young rabbits tells stories on the lawn—ridiculous, but nice to listen to, is my opinion. Sometimes."

Piper looked at me and opened his beak.

"If you don't like them, *I'll* tell you stories. I have a good one about the time I pecked a cat. Another about the time I stole a hazelnut out of a human's hand. I'm brave, have I made that clear?"

"I think I'm going to go," said the jay.

"No! Please. There's no one like me in the whole meadow. No one like me. No one."

Blue's pleading followed her as she rose swiftly into the canopy of leaves and disappeared.

"Hen's teeth," he muttered.

Now, I'm not saying I felt bad for that horrid bird as he sat alone on his branch. But I knew what it felt like to have sisters and brothers, who stood by me even if they didn't always understand me. And now I had two good friends. I'd never really thought about how every day of his life, Blue . . . had no one.

"Start hopping," Piper whispered to me. He flew in a circle and chirped a few notes of a tune. "Nothing like a stroll and a song on a sunny day, eh, Butternut? Oh, hello there, Blue! We finally made it to the stream, and our throats are thirsty. Would you like to draw near for a drink?"

Blue let out two mean screeches and flew into the forest.

I spoke first. "I know what you're going to say. *All creatures crave company*. But to make a friend, you need to have goodness inside of you, don't you? Blue has no goodness."

Piper was hopping around as if it were raining worms. "Incorrect! Do you know who has unlocked the tiny treasure box that contains Blue's goodness?"

I was confused. "You?"

"You! He has eavesdropping ears! He loves your stories, Butternut!"

"He called them 'ridiculous.'"

"That's just Blue being Blue. He's *listening*."

"He almost broke your beak, in case you've forgotten," I said. "He ate—"

"I have an idea." The glint in Piper's eye was unmistakable. "Just keep telling your tales, my creative companion."

Grandmother Sage always says that the stories she heard in the human house were her salvation and her path to truth. But . . . my stories hadn't changed Blue at all. He was as big a bully as ever.

"Be careful with Blue," I warned Piper. "Even if he has a tiny treasure box of goodness, the rest of him has been filled with mold and grime for years."

XVII.

We have come to it. No, not the rescue. My road test. Do you need a nibble? Do you need to relieve yourself?

No? Well, be warned. If your stomach is empty, you might keel over in a weak faint when you hear this part of the story.

Oh, that's right. I forgot. You already know how this part ends.

Well, please excuse me while I take another bite of grass. *I* don't want to faint while I tell the parts you don't know.

That's better. All right. Here I go.

Do you remember the weather? The day of my road test was an average day. Cool, but not too cold. Grayish cloud cover but no rain.

I couldn't eat a bite of breakfast. Piper tried to cheer me up. "Not one but two, not one but two," he chirruped. "*Two* surprises for you! You will excel at your examination. That's Piper's promise!"

He wouldn't tell me what the surprises were but seemed so confident. It helped a little. It also helped that Blue ate his breakfast and flew off that morning without incident. Maybe I wouldn't have to worry about him . . . and my only worry would be bone-crunching vehicle tires.

Thistle, Goosegrass, and I were testing that morning. I volunteered to go last. Grandmother once told a story about a tornado that transported a female human to another world. Maybe, before I had a chance to cross, a funnel cloud would whirl through Milkweed Meadow and do the same to me. The skies were gray, after all.

Because she hadn't been able to finish last time, Thistle wanted to go first. She looked both ways, stiffened her ears, and bounded across the road before Mother had stopped giving instructions. In a blink she was on the other side. We cheered her quietly, and she did a funny leap-spin to celebrate.

I wished I had her spunk.

Goosegrass was nervous, I could tell. Her head swiveled back and forth. "You can do this, my daughter," Mother said. "You are in control. Go when you know you can make it across. Trust your instincts."

Goosegrass kept looking both ways with frantic eyes. What Mother didn't appreciate was that a rabbit's instinct told us to turn *away* from the road and dash straight to the slumber nest.

A caw. We all looked up, and there was our meadow's menace, right on cue. His white belly gleamed against the grayness as he circled above us.

"Fancy rabbits crossing the road!" Blue called down. "Think they're too fancy to get flattened. They are *wrong*, is my opinion!"

His gaze traveled from Thistle to Goosegrass to me. I prayed for a tornado to take me.

"Run home and tell your stories, rabbits. The human vehicles will squash you like stink bugs. Then, poof! Silence." With these words, he began plummeting toward Goosegrass.

"Not today, Blue!"

I don't think anyone else heard music in that moment, but I swear to you, a harmonic chorus filled my head as if all the meadow's katydids, crickets, and grasshoppers had burst into song.

It was Piper. With an army of birds. They flapped toward Blue. They surrounded him. They drove him back into the sky.

Windy and Beaker were there. Skeet and his brothers. Amelia and her sisters. Tori and Efron. Vincent and Anjali, the woodpeckers. Mother and Father Firstfledge. Mother Firstfledge looked especially terrifying.

Let me put that another way. Blue looked especially terrified of Mother Firstfledge.

Like a swarm, the flapping birds held Blue at bay. "Go, Goosegrass!" Piper chirped.

She went. She passed her road test.

In that moment my fear left me. My sisters were dancing together on the side of the road in celebration. Piper, the kindest, dearest bird in the world, had convinced the other birds to protect us from Blue's harassment.

I had to summon my courage. If he'd done this for me, I could cross the road for him.

I approached the edge. Suddenly Piper dipped down alone to me. He murmured into my ear: "The second surprise. Find it in the forest."

I turned. At first I couldn't see anything but trees. Then I saw something bright and blue flapping between two trunks. I squinted at it.

It was Winsome's shiny blue ribbon. In Winsome's mouth. She was nodding her head, waving the ribbon. My second surprise!

She was cheering me on too.

I stepped into the road boldly. Mother was talking in reassuring tones to me, but I no longer needed her encouragement. I was Butternut: trellis climber, fawn rider. And now: road crosser.

I was in the middle of the road when I felt the ground vibrate beneath my paws. The pitch of my mother's voice heightened. A growl in the distance amplified.

A vehicle was coming.

I didn't pick a direction; I just ran. My mother, my brothers, my sisters, Piper and the birds all shouted at me, their strands of advice tangling into useless knots of noise. I ran and ran and wondered why there was still pavement under my paws, why I hadn't reached dirt and grass. Was the road expanding, growing as wide as it was long? The vehicle roared past me, huge and insolent, and a voice in my head told me I could stop. My legs didn't listen.

I thought of Winsome racing Piper. I thought of the way rabbits ran like deer. I was a deer now, long-legged, fleet-footed.

Piper later told me that he flew above me on the road for a while, shouting at me to turn around. I don't remember this. He told me Blue broke away and began following me as well, and Piper turned to divert him.

I ran until the birds and rabbits pursuing me grew weary and stopped to catch their breaths.

I ran until I made the very bad discovery.

I smelled it first: the tinny, tangy smell of blood.

I saw it next: dried blood smears and fur clumps on the pavement. A vision from one of my mind's brambles, brought into the world.

The faces of my family crowded into my mind's eye—Mother, Goosegrass, Kale, all of them. Was I looking at rabbit's blood? Whose absence would carve a hole in my life?

I forced myself to look again—and something inside me twitched in recognition. It was a sad and sorrowful thing, but it wasn't a rabbit.

The fur in the road was tawny gray.

I couldn't run through the remains. I collapsed where I was, closed my eyes, and shut my senses off.

I still don't know how much time passed while I crouched in a quivering ball. It was a warm touch on my belly that startled me back to my senses. For the second time in my life, another creature transported me. Two human hands lifted me gently into the air and carried me away from the blood and the fur.

Instinct made me wriggle.

"Don't worry," said a familiar human voice. "I'm bringing you back to your family."

Eventually I was set down on the lawn near the meadow. Near my burrow. I'm embarrassed to say that I didn't look behind me. I simply scampered home, to the loving clucks and nose rubs from my brothers and sisters who had returned to wait for me; from Grandmother Sage, who wanted the story when I was ready to tell it; and later from my mother and the rest of my siblings when they returned from looking for me.

When he spotted me in the root room, Kale barreled toward me like a tumbleweed.

"Oh, Butternut, I was so frightened. Thank goodness, thank goodness," he kept repeating while rubbing my nose.

I didn't thank the set of hands, nor the human to which they were attached, for carrying me home that day. I should have.

Although I thought I knew the answer, I asked Mother if running down the road and coming back alive was enough to pass the road test.

Her brow furrowed but her voice was gentle. "I imagine the road must seem more frightening to you than ever now. But learning not to panic is part of the test. You must anticipate danger and avoid it. We will test you again."

"Tell me what happened, Butternut," my grandmother asked, her weak eyes searching my face.

So I told the story, not quite as I am telling you now. I ended with the blood and fur in the road. I ended with the announcement that a coyote in Milkweed Meadow had been killed.

In my story, I said I ran home. I didn't mention the human, because rabbits don't trust humans. I knew Grandmother would say I was lucky not to be locked in a cage. I knew Mother would hurry us back inside every time the two small humans came to the window of the house near the meadow.

Because the voice that had reassured me and the hands that had carried me belonged to the little female human, the one who had sat at her open window and had been so forlorn the night Winsome broke her leg. And something told me that Grandmother and Mother were as wrong about her as they were about milkweed. I *could* trust her.

XVIII.

More than once a night, I dreamed about the coyote. In one dream her body was furry, but her face was a skull with hollow eyes and bared fangs. In another my squirrel friends Twain and Inka hung from her, squealing in futility, their tail fur stuck to dried patches of blood in her coat. I woke up shivering and moaning. Goosegrass snuggled into me. To my surprise Kale moved his sleeping spot near mine too. He woke up every time I did and clucked at me gently until I settled.

Sometimes the coyote was her old, unharmed self. She simply gazed at me as she stalked around the garbage bins. In one odd dream, under silver clouds, she curled her body around me on a chilly night and warmed me.

Now that she and her babies didn't threaten us anymore, mealtimes and playtimes should have been relaxed and joyful. But I'd seen what I'd seen. It was complicated.

Winsome understood. "That moment my leg snapped. It stays with me," she said. "Sometimes I'm running fast, and I remember it. I stop short and search the ground for burrows. Sometimes I dream about it too. Not always, but sometimes."

"We're by your side, Butternut," said Piper.

I did have a distraction. Piper told me to get to breakfast early one morning, but he didn't say why. I'd had a particularly *nice* dream about a clover field the night before, and I tried not to grumble as I hopped out while the sun was spilling its long beams on the lawn.

Blue was on the feeder ledge. He was stabbing open a peanut shell with his beak. The delight on his face as he chipped off little bits and ate them almost made him look pleasant.

Two other peanuts rested on the ledge.

He noticed me watching him. I thought he might make a crack about my road test, but all he said was, "Stay away from my peanuts, rabbit!"

"I don't like peanuts. And my name is Butternut," I said cautiously.

He dug into the second peanut. "I know that."

I didn't say anything more, and neither did he.

I took a mouthful of dewy grass and looked around for the face I knew was also watching Blue. Sure enough, there was Piper on the trellis, perched next to the stash of peanuts he had hoarded in his old nest, grinning like a fool. He nodded at me and flew away.

The following morning at dawn, Piper told me he watched Blue enjoy three more peanuts at the feeder. I chose to stay in my nest.

The morning after that, Piper told me to drag myself outside. I did—no peanuts. Blue sat on the feeder, alert.

"Up early again, you," he said.

"Yes."

"Forgetful humans forgot my peanuts."

I wondered if I should tell him that the humans had nothing to do with his precious treats. Before I could decide, Piper glided in a graceful circle above us and dropped a peanut on the feeder ledge next to Blue. "A merry morning to you, Blue!" he trumpeted. "Please pardon me for being late with your legumes."

Blue's eyes widened as Piper returned to his old nest and retrieved a second peanut, which he placed next to the first. "Bon appétit!" He then got a third peanut and began to peck into it on the ground next to me.

Since Piper wasn't paying him attention, Blue regarded me with his nightshade eyes. Once I'd quaked in fear under that stare. Now I was braver.

For Piper's sake, I swallowed my desire to call him cruel and friendless. For Piper's sake, I smiled.

Blue's face softened. He ate his two peanuts, while Piper finished his one.

Afterward Piper sighed. "Delicious. Blue, I have a single peanut left," he called as he flew to the nest and retrieved it. He placed it between them on the feeder. "One shell, two seeds. Two birds." He cocked his head. "What do you say? Shall we share it?"

To be honest, Piper didn't give Blue time to answer. He broke open the shell with his beak, rolled one of the seeds over to the jay, and bit into the other.

Blue didn't steal Piper's piece or push him off the ledge. The big brute actually shared. He and Piper ate their pieces side by side. With a "Farewell, friend!"—directed at Blue, in case that's not clear—Piper flew off into the morning sky.

Blue looked at me again. This time his gaze danced awkwardly. "Well. Stuffed, is my opinion," he muttered, and alighted into the oak canopy.

It was the first morning since my road test that I felt content eating breakfast. As the sun curved in its arc, heating my fur, the other birds slowly awoke and attacked the unguarded feeder seed with delight.

Don't get too warm and comfortable. It's finally here. The discovery that led to the great rescue. And to Piper's greatest disappointment.

XIX.

I was drinking from the stream at dinnertime when
Piper flew down and began whispering in my ear.
"Winsome's found something. She says it's an emer-
gency. Can you come?"

"Now?" I looked around. My brothers and sisters
were taking long, quenching drinks; some were still
eating. Mother, fortunately, was near our burrow
entrance. I figured I had a little time. I thought about
asking Goosegrass to cover for me again, but her guilty
look might raise Mother's suspicions. "Quickly," I
said. "I have to be home before bedtime to hear the
story in the slumber nest."

Winsome was waiting at the forest's edge, her
face solemn. "It's terrible," she said as she led us in
the opposite direction from her clearing. "I went back
to the fallen tree to see if there were any mushrooms

left—and I saw them." I kept careful track of our route in case I needed to hurry home. My mind's brambles snaked toward our mysterious destination. What would we see? What was so terrible?

Winsome stopped and pointed with her nose. A thick beech tree was lying on the ground. From the looks of the crumbling bark, it had fallen a while ago. Beneath a portion of its rotting trunk, there was a partially concealed den. In the den creatures nearly my size huddled together in an overlapping mass.

The creatures didn't shift when we drew close. They barely moved at all. They had meager fur coats, which didn't conceal the way their skin stretched over their spines and rib bones. Little bugs crawled in their fur, even over their closed eyes.

I counted seven.

"They're coyote pups, aren't they," I whispered.

Winsome nodded. "I think so."

For once Piper was silent, but he looked as if his heart had broken.

Winsome sighed. "They're so sad looking. I had to show you. I couldn't bear it alone."

So the mother coyote must have given birth to her litter before she met her tragic end on the road. I remember feeling in that moment that the next thing any of us said would matter a great deal. Would we be resigned to the pups' fate—as a sad and sorrowful part of life in Milkweed Meadow?

"We need a strategy to save them," announced Piper. "Begin brainstorming."

"But they're coyotes," said Winsome. "They'll grow up to eat Butternut and me—and you, if they can catch you. I don't know if we should do anything. Or even if we *can* do anything."

Piper went on as if he hadn't heard her. "Let's see . . . they need milk. How might we get them milk?"

Winsome and I looked at each other in bewilderment. Only another nursing coyote would provide milk for a litter of pups. If she existed in the meadow, we didn't know about her—nor would we live if we asked her for help.

"I think we might just have to be here for them. Sing them a song—or maybe you could tell them a story, Butternut. And then let them go," said Winsome quietly.

"Unacceptable," replied Piper, shaking his head. "We must try to transport them to safety."

Winsome frowned. "Where? How?"

"I have an idea," I said. My friends stared at me.

Sometimes storytellers tip the facts a little crooked. I could tell you that I was a hero. That I was as bighearted as Piper in wanting to save the abandoned, helpless coyote pups, and that my plan formed in my big heart. The truth is different. I wasn't sure at that moment that saving the coyotes was the right thing to do. If they grew up and made their home here, our forest visits would probably end. I might be frightened for the rest of my days.

But the plan in my mind was flawless. Three animals, three talents. Once I'd thought of it, I had to speak it aloud. And then once I'd spoken, well . . . I couldn't take it back.

"Piper, you spend the rest of the day weaving a nest strong enough to hold a pup," I began. "I'll meet you both back here tonight, and I'll push one pup at a time into the nest. Then we'll push it onto Winsome's back. I'll hold the nest in place while Winsome carries it to the humans' back door. We'll make seven trips. Then we'll peck and paw the door until the humans open it and notice the pups. The little female human will make sure they get milk. I know it."

From Piper: "Butternut, you are a genuine genius."

From Winsome: "The humans won't help! They hunt deer. They cage rabbits. Do you really think they're going to look at seven sickly coyote pups and want to save them?"

I thought of those gentle hands around my belly. "I do."

"They didn't help me," she muttered.

"They wanted to," I said. "Would you have gone with them?"

She didn't answer.

"You had a parent to protect you," said Piper. "You weren't in danger of dying. These pups may expire tonight if we don't do something. What do you say, Winsome?"

She looked at the pile of pups crisscrossed over each other, their tiny chests barely rising and falling. "Find me when the moon is out," she said, before trotting away.

"Your idea is inspired, Butternut." Piper was already hopping around, amassing a pile of twigs. "Tonight, we save seven innocents."

"I'd better get back." I took a last look at the pups and tried not to think about the long-snouted, jagged-fanged creatures they would grow into. I hoped we were doing the right thing.

XX.

I wish things had turned out differently.

There's a twist here. It changes the climax of my story.

Maybe you saw it coming, and maybe you didn't. It depends on how many stories you've read. And whether you like to make predictions, or to hand control over to the storyteller and let her float you along the river of her tale.

Narrative twists are fun because they surprise and unsettle you. And believe me, the climax—the rescue that set all of Milkweed Meadow abuzz—is still exciting. Perhaps even more exciting than it would have been.

But I lost a friend that night. While my story might be better for it, my life isn't.

When Piper and I approached the fallen tree, we were ready. He wouldn't stop talking about the nest he had built lightning-quick, how tightly he'd threaded the twigs into each other, how he'd stuffed the cracks with plant fluff and moss. I was ready to do my part too. To ride Winsome and steady each pup in the nest until all seven were at the humans' doorstep.

We knew something was wrong as soon as we arrived because there was a large creature lurking in the shadows just a few paces away. Piper and I froze—until he whispered that he thought it was a deer, and I whispered that I smelled Winsome's mother.

From the felled tree, Winsome beckoned to us.

"Mother and I are moving on," she said. Her lashes fluttered as she blinked in the moonlight. "I'm here to say goodbye."

We stood in silence, disbelieving. "No," said Piper.

"We'll try to join up with a herd now. My leg has healed, and I'm strong enough."

"Is this about the coyote pups?" I asked.

Winsome let out one of the long sighs we'd come to know well. "Even one coyote is too much for a deer. I can't save seven. I don't want to. I'm surprised you do, Butternut. This time you have real reason to be afraid."

"If we might speak to your mother—" began Piper, turning toward the figure in the shadows.

"It's not her decision. It's mine. You both are so lovely, but it isn't realistic that we'll stay friends forever. Robins need to worry about robins. Rabbits need to worry about rabbits. That's the way of things."

An old insult pricked at my memory like firethorn. "Do you mean rabbits?" I glanced hard at Winsome's mother. "Or hopping moss clumps?"

"Oh, Butternut."

"It is *not* the way things have to be," sputtered Piper.

"I'll never forget the way you helped me. And cheered me up. And Butternut, I'll miss your stories." She lifted something from the ground with her teeth and placed it, fluttering, at Piper's feet. It was her blue ribbon, whose cheery color seemed out of place in the gloom of the moment. "Here," she said. "Since the rescue nest will be of no use tonight, use this for your breeding nest when the time comes."

Piper's voice cracked. "A generous gesture, but I don't want your ribbon. I want you to stay."

I grasped at something that would keep her here. "You love the oak forest, Winsome. Stay with us and enjoy its beauty."

My words had exactly the wrong effect. Winsome got a dreamy look in her eyes. "I do love the forest, but there's beauty everywhere. I'm going to see more of it."

We looked at Winsome, Piper and I full of more sadness and sorrow than we could bear. "I won't forget you. Take care of yourselves, friends," she said, and turned away.

"Wait!" I stamped my front paw heavily three times on the forest floor. "Remember our scouting game? Come back. When you do, leave us triple hoof markings that point toward your location so we can find you. Please?"

She sighed again. "I can't promise I'll return. But if I do, I'll make it so we find each other, one way or another."

Winsome and her mother trotted away into the trees, her gait on her healed leg strong and sure.

The night sounds of the forest filled the silence between us.

"She might regret leaving and then return," said Piper at last, "like that lonely field mouse in your story."

"I don't think so." The hopelessness of the situation blistered inside me, as if I'd eaten a poisonous plant. Winsome was gone. She was truly gone.

I wanted to sit a while longer in my haze of self-pity, but I couldn't ignore the seven tiny creatures in the hollow beside us clinging to life. "Well," I said. "Shall we begin?"

Piper turned. "Begin what?"

"Helping the pups."

Piper narrowed his eyes and let out a screech of a laugh. For a startling moment, he looked like Blue.

"I can't carry more than a cashew. What do you propose, rolling each pup down a forest path? They wouldn't survive the journey." He hopped onto the large nest he'd constructed with such care, yanked out a twig, spat it away—and then rose into the air. "We can't help them without Winsome," he called behind him as he flapped back toward the meadow. "Perhaps she has a point. Why save carnivorous canines that will devour us for dinner?"

The answer entered my mind, true as the stars. Because these weren't carnivorous canines. They were newborn orphans, and we couldn't know about them and let them die. Because what kind of creatures would that make us? I felt a tiny shiver of righteous indignation, that same feeling I'd had when Blue snatched Grandmother's comb. Winsome was cowardly for leaving. I might always be a tangle of nervous brambles . . . but I wasn't a coward.

And Piper still believed in the goodness of every creature. He just needed reminding.

I gave chase. I couldn't beat a robin in a race, but that night, I came close. I called after Piper, who never flew completely out of sight but who seemed to be processing Winsome's departure by zooming in wild circles around the treetops. He ignored me.

When we reached the meadow's edge, I yelled, "Piper, I will chase you all night if I have to! You are wasting time! Get down here!"

Languidly he descended. He hopped over to me but kept his eyes on the ground. "She left us, Butternut." I'd never heard his voice quaver before.

I put my paw lightly on his foot and cleared my throat. "There were once a robin and a rabbit," I began. "They were best friends. The robin taught the rabbit that when creatures help each other, they live better lives. The rabbit taught the robin that not every creature would answer the call to help others, and that was okay.

"One day, they faced insurmountable odds. Seven coyote pups were sick, and time was short. The rabbit, who was used to changing the endings of stories, came up with a fresh plan. When he heard it, the robin leaped to his feet and exclaimed, 'Yes! As I've always said, a crumb of collective action, and we're all winners!'

"'I learned that from you,' replied the rabbit. So they rescued the pups and lived their best lives in Milkweed Meadow. The end."

Slowly Piper lifted his head. "Butternut, most faithful of friends, forgive my fickleness. What must we do now? Explain everything in that brilliant brain of yours this instant."

I did. And the rescue began.

XXI.

The bravest thing I ever had to do was not to climb the trellis, or cross the road, or ride on Winsome's back. It was to march into my burrow in the middle of the night, wake up my family, and beg them to help me save some young coyotes.

Please pardon me, but I've overheard you ask your father or mother for a favor from time to time. A second dessert. Extra playtime. The bigger the favor, the more nervous you are, wouldn't you say? And the likelier they are to say no.

So you understand that my task wasn't easy.

What gave me courage was the thought that this favor wasn't for me. It was for the pups. I tried to keep an image of them in my mind as I took a deep breath and squealed as loudly as I could in the slumber nest. My brothers and sisters popped their sleepy heads up, swiveling them from side to side. Baby Sweetcorn gasped and immediately began hopping up and down. "What is it, Butternut? Flood? Fire? Deer hoof through the ceiling again?"

"Meeting in the root room, now!" I announced. On my way out, I thumped on Goosegrass's ear until she woke up. If tired enough, that kit could sleep through a midnight lawn mowing. Honestly.

My nine siblings shuffled into the root room, followed by my mother, who demanded to know what was going on. My grandmother entered as well. "Butternut, are you unwell?" she asked.

I took a breath and told the most important story of my life. How seven orphaned animals were in a den in the woods on the verge of death. How our only chance was to get them to the humans' house before morning. How Piper was, at this very moment, rallying other animals to help. How the plan wouldn't work unless at least three other rabbits came with me. Even better, seven. Even better, everyone. How yes, the animals in need were coyote pups, but they were abandoned babies first and foremost, skeletal and infected with parasites. How I loved my family but didn't want to preserve our colony while ignoring other creatures. How I hoped I would get some help because I'd be going back out to save them no matter what.

I stopped. I waited, trying to keep my nose high and look more confident than I felt.

"My dear kit, you have taken leave of your senses." Grandmother Sage hopped forward from the entrance hole, blinking at me. "Coyotes. Humans. The forest at night. This nonsense is over. We will all return to sleep."

"I won't, Grandmother," I said. "And I've been in the forest at night many times." I glanced at Kale, who was staring hard at me. "It's dangerous, but I'm still here."

Mother's face filled with anguish, and I felt guilty for deceiving her. "You were one of the most cautious rabbits, Butternut," she said. "What happened to your milkweed? That robin has filled your head—"

"Please don't blame Piper. This is my choice. Please." I looked around at the faces of my brothers and sisters. "Can you honestly say you care about no creatures other than rabbits? Goosegrass, when those squirrels' tails were tangled together, you ran and got a comb to help them. It was the right thing to do. *This* is the right thing to do. Will nobody help me?"

"I forbid it," said Grandmother Sage. "I did not escape from captivity to see a branch of my colony decimated in a single night. Nettle, order your kits back to their slumber nest."

There was a long silence. I had thought my arguments might possibly persuade my grandmother—

after all, she had once been adventurous. She loved a good story too, and the rescue would provide just that. My mother was the stern one. I wondered why she wasn't marching us all back to bed.

"I appreciate your desire to help," my mother said finally. "But *coyotes*. We know how that story ends— with bloodshed and terror too frightening to talk about. It is simply too dangerous, Butternut."

"Excuse me, Mother." Kale's voice shook a bit as he spoke up. "But Butternut is talking about helping creatures in need, isn't she? And—isn't that what our stories teach us to do? If she's going no matter what, I'd rather she had some help than go alone."

Oh, Kale. I felt like nuzzling my eldest brother. "Exactly!" I exclaimed. "Sometimes we have to rethink the villains and heroes in our stories, don't we? We have a chance to be heroes tonight."

"Heroes—ha!" Grandmother Sage hopped toward me, her old eyes squinting at my face. "Do you know what I saw the night I came to Milkweed Meadow?" Her voice turned low and flat. "A band of coyotes attacked a litter of rabbit kits in front of me. Tiny, helpless babies in a shallow nest. As I hid, they devoured them, grinning, with blood on their muzzles. I remember the sounds, the awful smell. That grisly encounter haunts me, even after all these years. You, Butternut, will not be a hero tonight. You will be *food* for these wretched creatures."

What my grandmother had seen confirmed my worst fears. I trembled at the fate of the poor kits. But my brambles didn't flare up. My resolve stuck. These coyote pups were *not* beasts with bloody muzzles. Grandmother Sage's story was not my story.

"The attack sounds terrifying, Grandmother. I'm sorry you had to witness it. But wait until you see how helpless the pups are. They have more in common with the kits in your story than with the adult coyotes. Piper and I have a good plan, and I won't let him down." I looked around at my wide-eyed brothers and sisters. "Please come with me."

"I will," Kale said quietly.

"If you're going, I'm going," said Goosegrass.

"I want to be a hero too!" declared Baby Sweetcorn.

I beamed at them.

"Nettle, this is madness!" my grandmother exclaimed.

"No," said my mother, solemnly shaking her head. "It's compassion. For rabbits and for other creatures. It's as powerful a truth as any." She shook her coat. "I'm coming with you, Butternut."

"Me too!" exclaimed Thistle.

"And me!" piped Chicory.

Every one of my brothers and sisters crowded around me, and I felt I might burst from love. I nuzzled their noses in thanks. "We have to hurry."

Kale took charge. "Line up, two by two. Look out for your buddy. Cluck if you sense danger."

"We will protect each other, Mother Sage," my mother said.

My grandmother shook her head and curled up on the root room floor. "Stay alive," she said weakly.

XXII.

Picture this.

Two long sticks jammed in parallel through Piper's rescue nest.

Two rabbits gently nudging the first sickly pup from the coyote den into the nest.

Four rabbits each biting down on a stick's edge and lifting. Carrying that pup quietly through the dark forest to the house.

Picture four more rabbits concealed by the door, waiting. Unloading the pup when it arrives and placing it on the stone landing. Hopping the rescue nest back to the den while the first team of rabbits rests.

Picture the second pup loaded up, and the team returning to the landing to continue the relay.

Picture Mother Nettle hopping alongside both teams of her offspring, eyes primed for danger, whispering encouragement.

Now picture squirrels swarming the shadowy groundcover. Inka and Twain—awoken by Piper—leading the command. Picture the squirrels locating acorn caps and other empty nutshells and piling them by the stream's edge.

Picture the night sky dotted with day birds. The larger birds—woodpeckers, cardinals, mourning doves, and robins—dipping nut caps in stream water and flying them to the coyotes' den. Picture three more squirrels stationed in the den, paws extended, guiding the caps to the pups' dry mouths.

Picture the smaller birds—chickadees and house sparrows—industriously eating bugs off the pups' fur.

The oak forest in Milkweed Meadow was alive that night, and I hope you can see it in your mind. I felt an invisible string tethering me to every creature. Bird, squirrel, rabbit, we worked for a single purpose.

Piper and I directed the other animals in whispers. I placed myself in the first relay group with Goosegrass, Chicory, and Mallow. It was hard work, holding a twig in your teeth and timing your hops to match your sister's and brothers' so the nest wouldn't jostle. The first coyote pup didn't move or murmur as we crossed the forest. It was probably for the best, though a sign of life would have been reassuring.

Even though there were four of us, my neck muscles ached by the time we reached the dark landing. Mother took the lead in rolling the coyote pup out of the nest while the rest of us panted. The second team of Kale, Thistle, Watercress, and Lavender bit down on the sticks and bounded back into the forest, Mother beside them. A gentle wind was blowing, and the air felt wet; mercifully, the rain held off.

Six more pups, but only three more that our team had to carry, I told myself. I felt grateful that all my siblings had come along to share the load.

Goosegrass nuzzled me. "Where's that fawn Winsome you visited?" she asked. "Is she helping?"

I shook my head sadly. "She and her mother left Milkweed Meadow." I wished Winsome could have seen our teamwork that night. It might have changed her mind.

It was on our team's second journey that the miracle occurred. Clover and Baby Sweetcorn placed a new pup from the den in our nest. I don't know if it was because the cups of water had revived him, but this one was letting out little whimpers. I was glad to hear his voice, but it was eerie to carry a whimpering creature through the forest. We hoisted up the rescue nest and headed for the house.

Something above me blotted out the moonlight for a swift moment. A flicker, that was all, but my fur instantly stiffened. I set down my corner of the nest and motioned for my sister and brothers to do the same. Above us the dark leafy branches swayed innocently. The coyote pup whined.

"What is it, Butternut?" whispered Chicory.

While my mind's brambles whipped like vines in a windstorm, we waited. No one else had noticed anything. Even my mother's face was merely curious as she studied the dense canopy.

"It's okay. It was just the wind. Come on." Mallow bit down on his stick.

It hadn't been just the wind, I'd have bet my tail on it. But all appeared calm, and the pup's soft crying was getting to me. I took one last look skyward and nodded. Once again my siblings and I heaved him up.

We had taken no more than a few hops forward when I heard three low, rapid hoots. This time, the sound hit all our ears. The rescue nest dropped from our mouths.

"Hide!" Mother shrieked, but it was too late.

Everything that happened next happened in a field mouse's heartbeat. The owl tracking us dove from the tree canopy, wings extended, talons stretching toward Goosegrass. We squealed. Goosegrass cowered.

And then . . . a flurry of dappled feathers burst forth from an elderberry shrub and shot toward the owl. Our savior screeched and flapped and caused the startled bird of prey to pull up and circle back.

"Help!" The throaty call resounded through the forest. "The meadow rabbits need help, is my opinion!"

Blue (for now you know it was he) was joined by Piper, Windy, Beaker, Culver, Vincent, Anjali, Tori, Efron . . . a storm of birds swirling in a ring around the owl, pecking, scratching, and cawing. It didn't take long before that owl decided we weren't worth the abuse and sought a quieter dinner elsewhere.

When it was over, the birds landed beside us to check that no one had been hurt. Piper patted my paw. "Are you all right? That must have been terribly terrifying."

I nodded. I couldn't stop staring at Blue. None of us could.

"Nice moves, Blue," said Amelia the house sparrow.

"You saved us," said Mother.

"Not a fan of owls. Sneaky beasts," said Blue. He scratched at the ground with his foot. "Plus, if the silly one got eaten, the storytelling one would tell only boo-hoo sad stories in the meadow. *Boring*, is my opinion."

"Blue," I said, "I will tell the best stories I can for the rest of my life. Thank you for saving my sister." I chanced a glance at Piper, who had an exasperatingly smug look on his face.

"I'd better stick by you furballs tonight," said Blue. "After all, I'm the bravest bird around."

"You positively proved that, friend," said Piper.

Blue cleared his throat. "Well. Hop to it, then."

Blue was as good as his word. He flapped above us during our relays, even when rain began to fall. He offered his own version of motivational messages: "Hop, two, three, four! Pick up the pace, rabbits! You're not going to rescue anything moving *backward*, is my opinion!"

He drove us all batty, but I didn't really mind.

That night, with the help of the birds and squirrels, my family members and I successfully transported seven coyote pups from the forest to the humans' house. Once Mother had rolled the last wet and wheezing pup onto the landing, we gathered on the lawn. My body throbbed, but my brain wasn't tired. We weren't finished yet.

XXIII.

The rainfall turned heavy as we caught our breath. My sodden fur stuck to my body. I shivered.

"Butternut," Piper shouted, blinking drops of water out of his eyes. "What is your shrewd scheme to wake the humans? Should we pound on the door together?"

I nodded. I had assumed the transport would be the hard part and with some quick taps of Piper's beak on the glass, the kindly little female human would come running.

I hadn't planned on the rain. The squirrels rapped, my siblings and I pawed, and the birds pecked. To my dismay we sounded like the rainfall around us. Even Anjali and Vincent, whose sharp beaks and sonorous tapping often echoed throughout the meadow, didn't bring the humans to the door.

The birds started to caw. We screeched. Nothing.

Thunder bellowed nearby. The night was due to get noisier, not quieter.

"Louder, everyone!" I looked at Piper in futility. "What now?"

Piper stopped chirping and cocked his head up at the house. He flapped into the air, the water skimming off his feathers, and returned to me. "Have hope," he called through the rain. "Do you happen to know which part of the house is the humans' slumber nest?"

I remembered a figure at the window above the first floor, silently scratching out a story. I gestured to the upper level with my chin. "That's where the little female human spends time, I think."

"Let me see if I can rouse her from her rest." He flew to the upper floor and tapped on the window. I hopped back to watch. The windows had some sort of covering on the insides; I couldn't see through them the way I could during the day.

Piper's beak tapped. *Peck-peck-peck. Peck-peck-peck.* Then more insistently. As the rain soaked my fur and skin, I wondered if we creatures of Milkweed Meadow had misjudged how deeply humans slept and how badly their tiny ears worked. Would we ever rouse them?

Would the pups, now drenched and shivering, make it through the night if we didn't?

Piper let out a frustrated chirp. He flapped away from the house, far away, until he was over the meadow. He glided in an arc and sped back toward the window. Until the last moment, I didn't understand his intention—when I did, I screeched as loudly as I could for him to stop.

I closed my eyes the moment he struck the glass. The thud echoed in my ears.

I opened my eyes to see Piper tumble down the slanted eave, bounce over the gutter, and drop onto the lawn a few hops from the landing.

I raced over to where he lay. We all did. He didn't move. His eyes were closed peacefully. I nosed his wet body.

"Oh no, no," murmured Inka.

"Piper!" I shrieked. "Wake up right now!"

He didn't respond.

I had no ideas. No alternate endings. The dreadful prospect of losing Piper knitted my brambles into a tight patch. I could only nestle close to my friend's body and quiver. "Wake up," I whispered again.

"Human!" Blue squawked, and we looked up. The little female human's face was at the window into which Piper had just crashed. I waited for her to notice us, but she squinted into the rainy night in bewilderment. She yawned.

"Hen's teeth! A silverfish has sharper instincts than these humans, is my opinion!" Blue cried.

"Make some noise!" my mother shouted.

The next thing I knew, the birds were rising and pecking at the little female human's window while her eyes grew round as allium globes.

The squirrels scurried up the drainpipe and raced over the roof shingles.

Blue plucked a large quartz peastone from the path. He flew to the trellis and hurled the stone onto the porch light. The bulb shattered. Loudly.

Lights inside the house came on. First on the upper floor, then on the lower. When the four curious humans opened the back door, my brothers and sisters fled. The squirrels scurried away, and the birds raced to the treetops. I couldn't blame them; my instincts screamed at me to run as well. But I couldn't leave Piper.

"What on earth?" The human father knelt and stared at the coyote pups. The mother and the two little humans peered over his shoulder.

"Is there a den nearby?" The mother looked out into the rainy night. She eyed the broken porch light and frowned.

"They look hungry," said the little female human. "We need to help them."

"Should I get a box from the garage?" asked the little male human. After a pause the mother nodded.

The humans began wrapping the pups in some kind of cloth and carrying them inside, one at a time. I still couldn't breathe. No one had noticed Piper. I began to cluck, but no one heard me.

I realized how fast the long-limbed humans were moving. In mere moments the rescue would be complete, the door would be shut, and Piper would be left to his fate on the lawn.

A threshold lay before me. Crossing it meant surrendering whatever milkweed I still had in me. Abandoning caution—permanently. Taking a leap of trust and faith.

For Piper, I could do it. For Piper, I did it.

I wriggled onto the landing. With my teeth I tugged on the cloth enveloping the little female human's leg. She looked down. Her eyes widened, but she didn't cry out.

Her gaze darted to her family members—busy transporting the pups—then back to me. "Yes?" she whispered. So softly.

A caw sounded from where Piper lay on the lawn. We turned. Blue sat there in the rain. He cawed again. I tugged again.

At last the little female human noticed Piper. She gasped, and together we ran toward him, the grass muddy and slick under our feet.

Before the little female human called to her family to come help rescue a hurt robin she'd found, before Piper was wrapped in a dark cloth and carried into the house, before the door was closed and I began the longest wait of my life, Blue leaned toward Piper's still head.

"Come back, friend," Blue murmured. "Creatures will miss you, and Butternut will miss you most."

XXIV.

The next morning my brothers and sisters were still sleeping when I stumbled out of the burrow with stiff muscles. The rain had stopped, but the ground squelched under my paws. Blue was on a high branch of the feeder tree, his belly large, his eyes drooping. A few other tired birds breakfasted at the feeder. They chirped greetings at me, and I bade them a good morning.

Piper was not among them.

He wasn't perched on the trellis. He didn't come flapping down from the oaks, asking for a story.

From the lawn I peered through the first-floor windows of the house. There were no humans visible, at least from my angle.

"No one has seen Piper." My mother hopped over to me. I wondered if she'd slept at all. She'd spent the night in the slumber nest, nuzzling each of us until our heartbeats slowed and our chatter about the rescue subsided into snores. "The humans are away. Grandmother Sage's guess is that Piper and the pups are with some kind of wildlife rehabilitator."

I tried to imagine Piper with a human who healed hurt animals. Grandmother had told us that the wildlife rehabilitator's dwelling smelled like predators. Creatures in cages barked or whined or cawed distressingly. But Grandmother had liked the rehabilitator's concern for her health. And she'd liked that he'd advocated for her freedom.

I didn't wish whining predators on Piper . . . but maybe they'd help revive him.

"Is Grandmother still angry?"

"She's happy we're safe," my mother said. "She wants to protect our family, Butternut, and she goes about it the best way she knows how."

I'd avoided my grandmother last night. The thought of confronting her scared me. She would see me, now and forever, as the reckless rabbit, the one who didn't follow her rules. I didn't regret asking my family to help rescue those pups, but it did change things between us.

"I'm proud of what you did," my mother continued. "And I found the tree- and trunk-dwellers to be remarkably bighearted and clever. They ought to have some interesting stories of their own, don't you think?" She smiled. "I wonder if we might ask them to share a few with us sometime."

It was a marvelous idea, but I didn't know if I could listen to any stories if my first and finest friend wasn't around. "Mother, do you think Piper is going to be okay?"

Her long whiskers tickled my ear as she leaned close. "Birds fly into windows all the time. Some are dazed for a while and recover. Some don't. Piper may be one of the lucky ones. Stay hopeful."

The image of his motionless body and closed eyes didn't fill me with hope, but I returned a small smile.

From the burrow's entrance, Kale emerged, followed by Thistle and Chicory. "Hello!" Chicory called. "Is Piper back?"

"Why don't you go get a drink?" Kale suggested when he reached me. "I'll talk to the rest of the family this morning."

I nuzzled him, grateful for the chance to escape. Instead of heading for the stream, I hopped past the garbage barrels and down the front lawn. I sat at the edge of the road, perked up my ears, and listened. A vehicle was coming; I heard its growl plainly. It zoomed past, and once its echo faded, I could hear nothing else.

I hopped across the road.

Safe on the other side, I looked back at the house, into which the humans had carried my friend the night before. There was the meadow, its milkweed tufts now standing tall with the spring beauties, chicory, and daisies, whose names I'd taught Piper. In the forest beyond, long-necked oak elders mingled with ambitious saplings. The forest, too, had swallowed another friend yesterday.

Suddenly I craved more noise than the low buzz of insects and rustling breezes. I missed my friends' voices. The loss hit me. I put my head down and let my feelings unravel messily.

A while later I lifted my head. The world was unchanged. The wildflowers were still swaying in the sunlight. Remarkable, life-changing stories about all types of creatures would unfold in and around the meadow, and it would be there, blooming and dying and blooming again.

I realized that, but for the daylight, I was seeing Milkweed Meadow as Grandmother Sage had when she approached the house and its grounds for the first time. It was a beautiful place for a colony of rabbits to live. A colony with elders who loved me and who would help me grow. With siblings who would play with me and share stories that healed me.

It was home.

I listened, looked in both directions, and hopped back across the road and up the lawn. The rest of my family was out of the burrow, chatting animatedly with the birds and squirrels about the previous night's adventures.

I found my mother.

"If it's all right with you," I told her, "I'm ready to take my road test."

XXV.

By the time most of my siblings had made it to the front lawn, I'd crossed the road and hopped back again. It was just as easy the second time. As in any good story, a transformation had occurred: I was an experienced rabbit now, one who knew that the world contained weightier ordeals than a quick and cautious hop across some pavement. A fair number of birds and squirrels swept around me afterward, offering soft congratulations. Nobody was jubilant, of course. We were all still thinking about Piper.

I couldn't yet bear the thought of sitting through morning lessons or confronting my grandmother. I tried to make breakfast last as long as possible. I kept glancing toward the house, waiting for the back door to open and for Piper to come soaring out. The broken shards from the porch light lay untouched on the ground.

We heard the rumble of the humans' vehicle out front. Many of the birds swooped over the roof, and some of my siblings snuck around the house to spy. Mother didn't stop them. I didn't move from the backyard. If the news was good, I'd hear it soon enough. If it was bad, I'd hold on to my hope for a hair's breadth longer.

Blue flew back over the roof, leading some other birds. "Humans are in the house," he squawked at me. "Carrying something, not sure what."

I caught movement inside the house. Where was the little female human? Where? I'd know Piper's fate as soon as I saw her face.

There. The little female human and her brother appeared at the window. They were smiling! And watching us. And not moving. No door opened. No sign of Piper, bursting outside with as much joy as the day he fledged.

What were they doing? They couldn't possibly look this happy if Piper had perished in the night. They wouldn't . . . they weren't *keeping* him inside the house, were they? Panic seized me.

"Strange," whispered Blue. "An idea! Tell me a story to pass the time?"

I glared at him and clenched my paw so I wouldn't scratch his beady eye. "Forget it, Blue. Mother,

Mother, you don't think Piper's a pet bird now, do you? Where is he?"

She looked solemn. "We may not get answers today. Let's return to the root room and calm ourselves with a nice trivia duel on weed species. Come, kits!"

I didn't understand what was happening. I mourned Winsome's loss alone, but Piper was beloved by every animal in Milkweed Meadow. The meadow-dwellers were moving on far too quickly.

Numbly I left the fresh morning air behind and traipsed with my brothers and sisters to the root room. What else was there to do?

Grandmother Sage was waiting for us in the root room entrance. She looked tired. She probably hadn't slept either last night, waiting for us to come home. Suddenly I wasn't afraid to see her. I yearned for her wisdom and comfort.

"Grandmother, the humans took my friend the robin when he got hurt last night." My fears tumbled forth. "That's what happened to you, isn't it? The humans healed you and then wouldn't let you go. Was I foolish to trust them? I'm sorry that happened to you. I'm sorry I didn't listen to you."

Grandmother Sage, the founder of our colony, leaned toward me. "If humans ever captured your friend, you, Butternut, would come up with a crafty rescue plan. And it would succeed. I would certainly disapprove"—although her face remained solemn, I could hear charity in her voice—"but it seems you kits are going to decide for yourselves what's worth fighting for. Perhaps that's the way it should be. In the human house, there were many stories about the way things change over time. About older traditions giving way to new ideas and new ways of living. I'd conveniently forgotten those truths. But you found them on your own, my dear."

Her words felt like warm sunlight on my fur.

"You won't need a rescue plan though. At least not for now." She looked up, and I followed her gaze. There, from the place where Winsome's foot had stomped a hole, the place newly repaired with a lattice of twigs, a blue ribbon dangled. A breeze curled through the tiny hole we left for light and made the ribbon dance.

"Lovely. Even with my old eyes, I can see the brilliance of that color," my grandmother murmured.

Winsome's ribbon. For an instant I thought Winsome had returned—but no, Winsome had given the ribbon to Piper before she left. In the forest. Then where had it gotten to? Nobody knew except Piper. And if it was here in the root room now, that meant . . .

"I believe that friend of yours is playing around with you," Grandmother Sage said. My brothers and sisters began to chitter.

"Piper told Inka where to find his ribbon!" Goosegrass was hopping around like a crazed katydid, the truth bursting from her. "She gave it to me! I snuck it in while you were outside! He's back! He's okay! Piper's okay!"

Her final words trailed me as I dashed out of the burrow entrance. There was Piper, hopping on the grass, alive as the meadow flowers, surrounded by Windy, Beaker, his parents, and an assortment of birds and squirrels. I wanted to tackle him in sheer delight, but I controlled my impulse in case he was still injured.

"Piper!" I knew the little humans were watching me, and could perhaps hear, but I simply didn't care.

His face flamed with pleasure. "Butternut!"

"You're back! You're all right! Well—are you all right?"

"Right as rain." He lowered his voice. "I woke up in a box in the humans' vehicle. *I*, Piper Firstfledge, rode in a vehicle! They took me and the coyote pups to another helpful human, who told them I hadn't broken any bones and I'd be feeling fine and flying in no time. They watched me there a while, just to be sure. I had a headache, but it's fading fast."

"Oh, Piper, I'm so happy. And the pups?"

He grinned. "Even better news. All seven of those cuddly canines made it. The human called in a whole team of humans to feed them and clean them. They looked considerably haler and heartier this morning when we left. Sadly we won't get to watch them grow up, as the humans decided to relocate them to a wider wood with coyote packs and plenty of prey. The little female human was persistent on that point."

We wouldn't get to watch the coyotes grow up—and they wouldn't be around to eat us either. I looked over at the two faces staring affectionately at us. The glass that separated us was unnecessary. The humans had been trustworthy and heroic. They couldn't keep us perfectly safe—nothing could—but they'd done right by us meadow creatures. They deserved our thanks, especially the little female human.

"But—why didn't you fly over to me right away?" I asked Piper. "I was so confused. Why did you wait until I saw Winsome's ribbon to let me know you were okay?"

Piper looked at me with those shrewd eyes of his and burst out laughing. "Prolonging tension makes for a superior story. I learned that from you, fearless friend!"

XXVI.

Now that Piper was safe, Grandmother Sage wanted to hear us kits tell our version of the coyote pup rescue story. She invited our aunts and cousins into our root room to listen too. Since his breeding-nest days were still far off, Piper told me I could keep the blue ribbon for now. We wove it into the ceiling, an ornamentation that my extended family admired when they arrived.

To my surprise, Grandmother asked Goosegrass to tell most of the rescue story. Nervously she began, and I had to bite my tongue when she told a few things out of order. But when she described my plan as "pure brilliance, something only the kindliest and cleverest rabbit in the world could have thought up," I hunched over with pleasure and embarrassment.

And no one, not even I, could have described the terror of the owl attack as she did.

Before we all broke up, Grandmother asked me to tell the story of the day I climbed the trellis and met Piper. "It is time for this brave rabbit's truth to be appreciated by all," she proclaimed, much to my delight. I enjoyed reliving my anguish and triumph. I think I knew Piper was special as soon as he greeted me openheartedly at the trellis top, eager for friendship.

"Please don't get any ideas," my mother begged of us kits. "Please try to keep your adventures on the ground."

After the rescue Blue still got to the feeder first in the morning and gobbled seeds to his heart's content. If other birds joined him, he no longer cawed or lunged at them but let them eat their breakfasts in peace. Well, *peace* isn't the most precise word, since he chattered at them constantly. "Good morning, friend!" he'd call. "How did you sleep? How are your eggs? Where is your brother? Did the bullfrogs' croaking keep you up last night? I heard an owl too, as I was drifting off. Probably the same owl that we drove away in the forest. Probably searching for the brave blue jay who robbed him of his dinner. Probably wants revenge. Ha! Just let him try to come after me, is my opinion!"

I think he was making up for years of loneliness. He was tiresome to listen to, but it was such an improvement over the old Blue that we all let him go on as long as he liked.

Mother Firstfledge refused to be friendly with him at first, but he flew after her one day and apologized relentlessly.

"Truly sorry I ate your egg. Shouldn't have. Hotheaded decision. Horrible. Will you be my friend if I promise never to eat any meadow bird's eggs again? I'm everybody's friend now—want to be yours too, Mother Firstfledge."

"Forgive him, Mother!" Piper was hovering nearby. "Blue regrets what he did!"

Blue nodded vigorously.

Mother Firstfledge stared him full in the face. "I will never forget that day. I will never know that little nestling of mine because of your impulsiveness."

"Ashamed. Awfully sorry. Would change things if I could, is my opinion," mumbled Blue.

"You may earn my forgiveness not only by leaving our eggs alone," she continued. "You must promise to *defend* the nests of the birds of Milkweed Meadow. If birds of prey come, if any snakes or crows get any wild ideas, you must fight them just as you fought that owl. Make up for your past with sheer effort, Blue. For the rest of your life."

He brightened. "Why, Mother Firstfledge, nothing would please me more. Just let any critter try to go after your eggs! I'll show 'em who's the boss around here."

Mother Firstfledge gave him a curt nod, which I guess was her way of forgiving him. "By the way, Blue, there is a jay by the stream who flew in for a visit this morning. For goodness' sake, go get yourself a mate."

Blue's mouth opened. "Er—much obliged," he stammered awkwardly. "That is—do you have any tips? I haven't had the finest luck—"

"Be kind. Don't boast. Listen more than you talk. Hen's teeth, it's simple, Blue!"

He nodded. "*Be kind. Don't boast. Listen more than you talk. Be kind. Don't boast. Listen more than you talk.*" He muttered Mother Firstfledge's words all the way to the stream. Piper and I didn't follow, so we don't know how that particular project of Blue's is going. Though spring's final days are behind us, the summer is full of possibility.

Piper and I like to visit Winsome's clearing and the coyotes' old hollow under the trunk. We look for patterns of three hoofprints on the ground. We haven't found any, but that doesn't mean we never will. I hope, wherever Winsome is, that she's surrounded by beauty and feels that she's found a true home as part of a herd.

I keep telling my mealtime stories, some about the meadow creatures having adventures together, many about humans and creatures magically interacting. The seeds for these stories have been freshly planted in my head, and I enjoy nourishing them into tales. My audiences seem to like them fine.

Even so, I've been feeling a kind of restlessness. I spoke to Piper about it. "After the excitement of the rescue, well . . . things just feel a little dull around here."

Piper hopped to and fro. "I've been feeling the same way! All I ever wanted was for everyone in the meadow to respect and rely on each other. Now we do. Sometimes I go to sleep and realize that my day was exactly like the day that came before it. Except for your singular stories, of course, friend."

"Without conflict, there's nothing to keep a listener listening to a tale. It's one of the first things we learned from Mother and Grandmother. Without conflict in life, things feel safe—but boring." I still worried about choking on clover or falling in the stream, of course. It wasn't that my brambles had withered entirely. But I'd grown a tiny bit affectionate toward them. They hadn't hindered me when things mattered most. And they would keep me watchful.

"But we are fools to seek danger for its own sake," Piper pointed out. "What if some creature got hurt? What if *you* got hurt? I'd never forgive myself!"

"Maybe we don't need a coyote. Maybe we just need something new to happen," I mused.

"Hmm. Something new. I like your logic. Something new . . ."

"Let's think on it."

Piper nodded in agreement.

I'll tell you the truth: I already knew what I was going to do. I'd had the idea a while back. I was going to make a new friend. Someone who already understood how much stories—and creatures—mattered.

Morning after morning I began leaving the slumber nest when the sky was turning from black to soft gray. The dew on the grass was still cold, the birds still roosting. I waited and watched.

Finally, one morning, *this* morning, I spotted the little female human, usually the laziest and last to appear by the first-floor windows, awake as early as I. And alone. I jumped up and down until she spotted me, as I knew she would.

She came outside and padded through the wet grass. Knelt in front of me. "It's you," she said. "Good morning."

I nuzzled her foot with my nose to start off on good terms.

She regarded me intensely, with eyes that gleamed in the gray dawn. "I know you brought those coyote pups to us. And led me to the hurt robin that night. I know it was you. I've heard you speak. No one believes me, but they don't listen the way I do. Tell me about it. Tell me how you rescued those pups."

And so, my friend, I did.

THE END

garbage
bins

trellis

feeder

blackberry brambles

road